MW01098101

Dead Horse

Also by Walter Satterthwait

Novels
Cocaine Blues (1979)
The Aegean Affair (1981)
Wall of Glass (1987)
Miss Lizzie (1989)
At Ease With The Dead (1990)
Wilde West (1991)
A Flower In The Desert (1992)
The Hanged Man (1993)
Escapade (1995)
Accustomed To The Dark (1996)
Masquerade (1998)
Cavalcade (2005)
Perfection (2006)

Short Story Collections
The Gold of Mayani (1995)
The Mankiller of Poojeegai and Other Stories
                              (forthcoming, 2007)

Non-fiction
Sleight of Hand (a critical biblio-biographical study
                              with Ernie Bulow, 1993)

Dead Horse

A Novel

WALTER SATTERTHWAIT

Dennis McMillan Publications
2006

FIRST EDITION
Published November 2006

Dustjacket design and interior artwork
by Michael Kellner.

ISBN 0-939767-55-4

Dennis McMillan Publications
4460 N. Hacienda del Sol (Guest House) Tucson, AZ 85718
Tel. (520)-529-6636   email: dennismcmillan@aol.com
website: http://www.dennismcmillan.com

This book is dedicated to the three Emilys

Dead Horse

from *The New York Herald, European Edition,*
May 26, 1935

OBITUARIES

WHITFIELD, Emily Davies Vanderbilt Thayer

By her own hand, at her ranch, Dead Horse, in San Miguel County, New Mexico.

Mrs. Whitfield had been a prominent society woman for many years, in New York City, Newport, and Paris, France. The daughter of the late Frederick M. Davies, the banker, broker, horseman and clubman, she married William H. Vanderbilt on November 1, 1923 in Grace Church, a wedding that was one of the notable events of the winter season. She and Mr. Vanderbilt were divorced in June of 1928, with Mr. Vanderbilt retaining custody of their single child, a daughter, Emily.

In December of that year, she married Mr. Sigourney Thayer, a theatrical producer. They were divorced six months later.

Over the next several years Mrs. Thayer lived in the U.S. and in France, where she traveled in literary and theatrical circles and was frequently a guest of the "modernist" American writer Gertrude Stein.

On July 19, 1933, in New York City, she married Mr. Raoul Whitfield, the popular American mystery novelist. Together, they moved to the American southwest, where they constructed a luxurious ranch near the town of Las Vegas, New Mexico. They hosted elaborate parties, their guests arriving from New York, Los Angeles, and various European capitals. In February of 1935, to the surprise of their friends, they separated. Mr. Whitfield moved to Los Angeles and Mrs. Whitfield filed for divorce, which had not become final at the time of her death.

On the morning of May 24, Mrs. Whitfield was found dead on her bed, her outstretched right hand holding a Colt .45 revolver. She had been shot in her left side. A coroner's jury brought in a verdict of suicide.

Mrs. Whitfield will be buried in New York. It is understood that Mr. Whitfield will not be attending the funeral.

from The San Francisco Examiner of Wednesday, September 30, 1942:

OBITUARIES

WHITFIELD, Lois Bell. Born September 9, 1915, died September 27, 1942, of injuries sustained in an accident. Beloved wife of Raoul Whitfield, scribbler, of Pasadena. She was raised in Las Vegas, New Mexico, but she was, once upon a time, very happy to leave it. "She walks in beauty, like the night. . . ."

From *The Pasadena Ledger* of Wednesday, January 26, 1945

DEATH NOTICES

Whitfield, Raoul, January 24. In the Veterans Hospital of Pasadena, of tuberculosis.

PART ONE
1935

CHAPTER ONE

H igher!" said Maria.
Tom smiled.

For as long as he could remember, she had thrown herself into things. Into situations, into life. One morning when Carla was feeding her careful spoonfuls of oatmeal, as slow and precise as a surgeon setting sutures, Maria had snatched the spoon from her mother's hand and slammed it at the cereal, splashing spurts of oatmeal and milk and butter across the table and down her pajamas.

Now it was the new swing set.

Well, not new. You couldn't buy a new swing set on the kind of salary that Tom earned.

But he had gotten it at a good price from the Gardiners – to their two kids, now in high school, the thing was an antique. Over the past few weeks, working in Mel Gardiner's garage in his spare time, he had sanded the metal tubing, primed it, painted it a glossy red. Yesterday, on Maria's tenth birthday, Mel had helped him move and reassemble it. And when she came home from school, he had led her out into the back yard.

She had spent the rest of the day demanding that he push her higher. And this morning she had been up early, fully dressed, shoving at his shoulder, "Daddy, wake up. Let's do the swing."

He stepped back from the swing. "Okay, Sweetie. You do it. But not too high."

At the rear of her arc, she leaned her body back, holding the chains tight in her small hands. She stuck out her legs and sailed down through the air, and then went swooshing up. She leaned forward, pushing the swing higher.

Today she was wearing a pleated red skirt and a pink blouse. Carla's favorite colors.

Was it some memory of her mother, of Carla's taste in clothes? Or did the two of them simply share the preference, something instinctual, something in the blood?

"Not too high," he said.

"I'm being really careful," she said.

She sailed down and up, forward, seemed to hover there for a moment, then sailed down and up, backward.

"Okay, Sweetie," he said. "Enough. You've gotta get ready for school."

"I am ready for school," she said.

"Your hair's a rat's nest."

She looked over her shoulder as she swooped away. "Rats are good."

"Rats are bad."

"I'll brush it. It'll take me a minute."

"Tom?"

A voice off to his right. He turned.

Carlos Obregon, one of the deputies, stood at the side of the house. Like Tom, he was wearing the beige uniform. On his head was a beige Stetson, a duplicate of the one waiting inside for Tom, on the rack by the front door, beside his gunbelt.

"Talk to you?" Carlos said.

Maria had been slowing herself down. Now, as the swing reached the bottom of its arc, she slid her foot against the grass.

Tom caught the chains and eased the swing to a stop.

"You go brush your hair, Maria," he told her. "I'll be there in a minute."

"But —"

"This is business, sweetie."

"Oh, well, okay." She jumped from the seat, turned around so he could see her pout – she was going, but not happily – and then flounced off to the back door.

Tom looked at Obregon. "What is it, Carlos?"

"I tried calling, Tom. No one answered."
"Can't hear the phone out here. What is it?"

• • •

Ten minutes later, Tom found Maria in her bedroom, standing at the window, staring out at the yard and the swing set.

"Okay, sweetie," he said. "Carlos'll drive you to school."

She frowned at him. "How come you can't drive me?"

"Business."

"What business?"

"You remember little Emily? Out at Dead Horse? Dead Horse Ranch?"

"She's not little. She's the same age as me." Concern tightened her small face. "Is something wrong with Emily?"

"No. It's not Emily."

"She's in France. With her father. Remember? I got a postcard from her, with that Eiffel Tower on it."

The two girls had met at the Fourth of July Parade last year, when young Emily was visiting her mother and step-father at Dead Horse, and they had exchanged addresses. For a while, after Emily returned to France, Emily and Maria had written letters to each other. But after several months the letters from France had stopped. Tom had once asked Maria, deliberately casual, if she'd heard anything from Emily, and Maria had said only that Emily was very busy in France. But she had been wearing the still, immobile face she wore when she was being brave; and he had wished, once again, that there was some way to protect your child, protect every child, from pain and loss.

"I remember," he said.

"So what's wrong out at the ranch?"

Probably, by the end of the day, the whole school would know, teachers and students both.

As gently as he could, he told her.

"Oh no," she said, her face stricken. "Does Emily know?"

"I doubt it. Not yet."

"Who's going to tell her?"

"Me, probably. I'll call her father."

8

She looked at him gravely for a moment. "You've got a really terrible job, Daddy," she said.

He nodded. "Sometimes."

She turned and stared out the window, toward the swing set. Her face was still.

"Listen," he said. "I'll see you tonight. You go over to Mrs. Gomez's house after school. I'll pick you up."

Without turning from the window, Maria said in a small, distant voice, "Mrs. Gomez smells bad."

"I'll talk to her about that. Do I get a hug?"

She turned and came to him, and he could see that the stillness of her face was about to shatter. She wrapped her arms around his neck as he bent toward her, and suddenly, against his cheeks, he could feel her tears, slick and hot.

CHAPTER TWO

Tom turned off Route 66 onto the reddish washboarded road that led to Dead Horse. The old Dodge passed between the gate posts and beneath the bleached white skull bolted to the crossbeam overhead.

It was the skull of a horse. He had heard the story somewhere: one of the Whitfields' workers had uncovered it during the construction of the main house, and Mrs. Whitfield had sent someone to plant it up there on the beam. She had named the ranch after it.

Something only an Easterner would do – flaunting the skull and naming a ranch after it.

Tom had been around horses for all his life. He had no great fondness for them – they were even more stupid, he believed, than dogs – but he admired their strength and stamina. Using a horse's skull as a kind of decoration seemed frivolous, belittling.

And naming the place after a dead horse – he wasn't a superstitious man, but he figured that any ranch with the word "dead" in its name was probably asking for trouble.

And now the trouble had arrived.

The sun was still climbing up the clear blue sky; the shadows of the piñon and juniper trees lay long and black across the road. There was no wind. On either side of him, the scrub brush and the pale green buffalo grass stood upright and unmoving.

Up ahead, behind a low ridge and moving toward the next bend, he saw a big blurred rooster tail of yellow dust swirling through the clear air. A car, probably two cars.

He slowed down and eased the Dodge as far to the right as he could get it without sinking the wheels into the ditch that bordered the road.

Around the bend came Jerry Baca's old Ford pick-up, jouncing on its worn shocks. Behind it came a dusty green Chevy sedan he didn't recognize.

Baca saw the county Dodge and abruptly he slowed the truck. The driver of the Chevy, caught off guard, nearly rammed the sedan into the Ford's bumper.

As the truck passed Tom, Baca gave him a slow, solemn wave.

Tom nodded to him, his mouth grim. He could feel an anger begin to build inside him.

Jerry Baca was the brother-in-law of Dr. Fleming, the county coroner, and somehow he managed to get himself assigned to every coroner's jury that Fleming put together. If he was leaving already, it meant that the jury had already finished its work. Had closed up shop even before Tom arrived to take a look at the scene.

• • •

Outside the adobe wall that encircled the main house, there were four cars parked: the county Dodge driven by Deputy Phil Sanchez, Dr. Fleming's black Chevrolet, a black Ford roadster owned by Peter Alonzo, the assistant District Attorney. The fourth car was a sleek black Packard that belonged, Tom knew, to Murray Carleton.

What the hell was Carleton doing here?

Tom parked his car and got out. He slammed shut the door, stalked down the flagstone walkway, through the gate and across the brilliant dark green grass. He stepped up onto the Territorial style portal and rapped his knuckles against the front door.

After a moment, the door was opened by Phil Sanchez, who moved aside to let him in.

"Jeeze, Tom," he said. "I'm glad you made it. It's been crazy here."

It was a typical Southwestern – rich Southwestern – entryway. Saltillo tiles on the floor, framed landscapes on the white-stuccoed adobe walls.

"It's all over," said Sanchez. "The coroner's jury –"

"Saw them on the road. Didn't waste any time, did they?" He looked around the hallway. "Where?"

11

"Down this way."

Tom followed him to the right, along the dark red tiles. Hanging on the wall were more landscapes.

As they passed an opened door on the left, Sanchez nodded toward it. "The foreman's room. Name's Chervet. Victor Chervet. A Filipino."

The were approaching a tall dark antique wooden door.

"Came in to light a fire in the fireplace," said Sanchez. "Like always, he says. Seven o'clock."

"He sleeps here in the house?"

"Guess so."

They reached the door. Sanchez grabbed the doorknob, turned it, pushed the door open, and stood back.

Tom took off his Stetson as he stepped into the room, into the female smell of perfumes and oils. Hovering behind them, faintly, a half-forgotten memory, was the smell of gun powder.

She lay on her back on the bed, her arms spread, a beautiful blonde woman in a red velvet dressing gown, her mouth open, her face slack.

He remembered her on the Fourth last year. Slim and athletic, squatting down onto her heels to give a cone of cotton candy to her daughter, her smile bright, her right hand resting on young Emily's shoulder. A breeze had ruffled the bright lemon-yellow silk of her dress, ruffled her fine pale hair. The girl, her eyes wide, had taken the candy solemnly, as though it was a gift of great importance.

They had the same name, mother and daughter.

Sometime today the other Emily would be learning what had happened to this one.

He looked at the bed. The dressing gown was spread open – fallen open? pulled open? – and beneath it she wore a pair of black silk pajamas. There were powder burns and blood on the left side of the pajama top, below her ribcage, above her hip, and more blood darkly staining the crumpled folds of gown. Beside her on the chenille bedspread, to the right, lay a long-barreled chrome-plated revolver, a Colt.

Phil Sanchez had moved into the room.

Holding the brim of his Stetson in his left hand, the hat along

12

his thigh, Tom began to move slowly around the bed, studying the woman.

"The foreman," he said. "Chervet. He didn't hear the shot?"

"The radio was on all night. She turned it on when she went to bed, he says. Around eleven. She always turned it on at night."

Tom glanced at the radio on the nightstand. Beside it, next to the electric lamp, stood a small medicine bottle. He stepped over to the nightstand.

"You print the bottle?" he asked Sanchez.

"One set on it. Hers, probably."

Tom picked up the bottle. "Luminal. Sleeping pills. Prescribed last week." Lightly, he shook it. "Almost full. Who's Dr. Hamilton?"

"The new guy. He took over from Dr. O'Brian."

Tom put back the bottle and turned to the woman. "Any windows broken?"

"No."

"Front door locked? Back door?"

"Both, Chervet says."

He nodded to the Colt. "Whose gun?" he said.

"Hers," said Sanchez.

"And it was there when Chervet found it? On the bed like that?"

"It was in her hand when he came in, he says. He took it out."

Tom looked at him.

"He says he was nervous, didn't know what he was doing."

"Where's he now?"

"He had things to do in town. Mr. Alonzo told him he could go."

Tom inhaled, exhaled. "Tell me you're pulling my leg, Phil."

"Jeeze, Tom, he's the District Attorney. What could I do?"

"For Christ's sake."

"Tom, I'm sorry, but he said it was okay."

His mouth tight, Tom turned back to the woman. "Prints on the gun?"

"Yes, sir. Hers, probably, and probably Chervet's."

"On the trigger?"

"All smudged up."

"You print Chervet before you let him go wandering off?"

"Tom—"

"You print him?"

"I printed him."

Someone knocked at the door.

Tom turned.

Standing in the doorway was Dr. Peter Fleming, the county coroner. Sixty-one years old, bald but for the furry white fringe above his ears, he wore a rumpled, inexpensive black suit. He had worn the same suit, or one identical to it, for years.

"Sheriff," he said.

"Doctor," said Tom. "What've we got here?"

"I should think that's obvious," said Fleming. "The woman committed suicide."

"She was left handed?" Tom asked him.

"Right handed," said Sanchez. "The gun was in her right hand, Chervet says."

Tom said to the doctor, "She's right handed and she shoots herself way down there on the left side?"

"I've seen it happen before," said Fleming. "People in extremis do some very strange things."

"She leave a note?"

"Suicides don't always leave a note." He added, "As you know."

Carla, Tom thought.

He felt anger again: a pressure against his chest, a tautness along his face.

In a flat voice, he said, "What do you mean by that, Doctor?"

Fleming blinked and seemed to contract slightly within the cheap suit. "I, ah, meant only that as a law officer, you'd know of course that many people don't leave a note. It happens."

"Uh huh."

"Sheriff, the jury has already made its decision."

"Didn't take 'em long."

"The facts are self-evident."

"Right."

Fleming glanced at the body, looked back to Tom. "Well. I'll be going. If you need me, I'll be in my office."

Tom nodded.

14

After the doctor left, Tom turned to Sanchez. "That big Packard outside. That's Murray Carleton's. How'd he get here?"

"Chervet called him."

"Why?"

"Carleton is Mr. Whitfield's lawyer."

"Where's Whitfield now?"

"California. Los Angeles, Carleton says. Been there since February. He and Mrs. Whitfield are legally separated."

"I heard," said Tom. He turned to look at the dead woman.

"She filed for divorce in February," said Sanchez. "Carleton says it wasn't final yet."

"Maybe not," said Tom. "But this is."

CHAPTER THREE

After sending Phil back to town, Tom went out to talk to the others.

Murray Carleton and Peter Alonzo, the Assistant District Attorney, were in the living room, Carleton sitting in a big brown club chair, his hands along the chair's arms, his right ankle on his left knee. His boots were made of shiny, hand-tooled leather. Handsome and elegant, in his late-thirties, he wore a light-weight gray three-piece suit, a thin gold chain slung from the center button of his vest to the watch pocket. His thick hair was black, theatrically gray at the temples.

Alonzo sat across the room on the matching leather sofa. He was twenty-eight years old, slightly overweight but hiding it well in a carefully-tailored suit of black wool. His tie was silk and, like Carleton, he wore expensive boots. His black hair was thin, combed over from left to right. He had the face of a politician, open and earnest. His eyes were brown; his mouth was small and plump.

"Tom," he said, and nodded.

"Peter," said Tom. "Mr. Carleton."

"Sheriff," said Carleton. "Take a seat."

Tom felt a flicker of irritation – Carleton offering him a seat in the dead woman's house? – but he pushed it aside. First, he told himself, find out what's going on here.

He sat down in the room's other leather chair, forming the third point of a triangle. Between the three men, a large pinto horse-hide rug spread out across the hardwood floor.

"A terrible thing," said Alonzo. "That poor woman. Why the hell would she do that?"

16

"Maybe the autopsy'll tell us," said Tom.

"Autopsy? Dr. Fleming's satisfied that she committed suicide. The coroner's jury's already made its decision."

"No note," said Tom. "Bullet hole's on the left side. She was right handed."

"The doctor has explained all that. The county won't pay for an autopsy, Tom. Not for an open and shut case like this."

"If she wanted to kill herself, she had enough Luminal in there to do it three or four times."

"The gun was faster," said Alonzo. "More certain."

Tom nodded. "I hear you let the ranch foreman go. Chervet."

"He was distraught. He needed to get into town, talk to his doctor. There was no reason to stop him."

"Last person to see her alive. Tampered with evidence. Moved that pistol."

"As I said, he was distraught. He was in shock, Tom."

"Anybody else in the house last night?"

"No. A friend of hers had been staying here. A Miss Templeton, from New York. But she left a few days ago, moved into the Plaza Hotel."

"You ask her why?"

"What's the point, Tom? She wasn't here last night. There's no way she could know what happened."

"There any ranch hands?"

"Two. But the bunkhouse is over a hundred yards away. They didn't see or hear anything."

Tom nodded.

Alonzo ignores the wound in the wrong side. He ignores the sleeping pills. He ignores the friend and he lets Chervet walk away. He runs the coroner's jury in and out, wham bang, in less than half an hour.

He turned to the other man. "Surprised to see you here, Mr. Carleton."

"I came as soon as I heard. Victor Chervet called me."

"And you called the Assistant District Attorney."

Carleton nodded. "Doing my duty, Sheriff, as an officer of the court."

"And you came out here yourself."

"I thought that perhaps I could do something."

17

"Like what?"

"I do represent her husband, Sheriff."

"In the divorce?"

"And in other matters."

"Thought he was out in California."

"All the more reason for me to be here, representing him."

"He need representing?"

"Everyone is entitled to representation, Sheriff." He smiled. "It's in the Constitution, I believe."

Tom nodded. "You happy with the idea of suicide?"

"Happy?" said Carleton, and frowned at the word. "I was very fond of Emily."

"Even though you're representing her husband."

Carleton lowered his right ankle from his left knee, hooked his left ankle over the right knee, stitched his fingers comfortably together across his stomach. "I've known them both for a long time. And I was fond of them both. That didn't change, merely because they were in the middle of a divorce. She was still a friend. And I was worried about her. I knew that she'd been despondent lately."

"Despondent?"

"She missed her daughter – Little Emily. She's living in France with her father."

Tom nodded.

"And this was her third marriage," said Carleton. "She was upset that things hadn't worked out."

"Why is that?"

"Why hadn't they worked out?"

"Yeah."

Carleton separated his fingers and lightly raised his hands. "Who knows? People change. They grow apart."

"Anything specific to make that happen?"

He shook his head. "So far as I know, it was a simple parting of ways."

"When's the last time you talked to her?"

"Emily? Yesterday."

"What about?"

"Nothing in particular. I telephoned to see how she was doing."

"She sound suicidal to you?"

"Obviously, if she had, Sheriff, I'd have come over here. But as I say, she did sound unhappy."

"Who inherits?"

"Pardon me?"

Alonzo said, "What are you getting at, Tom?"

"Simple question," Tom told him. He turned back to Carleton. "Who inherits? The ranch. The money. She had money, right?"

"Yes."

"And they're still married? Legally?"

"That's correct."

"She have a will?"

"I believe so."

"New one?"

"Not so far as I know. But I'm his lawyer, Sheriff, not hers."

"Who's hers?"

"Bradley Benson in Santa Fe."

"You talk to him lately?"

"A few days ago."

"He mention anything about a new will?"

"No."

"So the odds are good that Mr. Whitfield gets it all."

"Tom," said Alonzo, "for God's sake, he's in California. He didn't come out here and –"

"He know about this yet?" Tom asked Carleton. "Her dying?"

"No." He pulled a gold watch from his pocket. "It's only seven thirty out there."

"You have his phone number?"

He raised his eyebrows. "You're going to call him?"

"If he's there."

"Of course he's there."

"Then I'm gonna call him. You have his number?"

"Yes. Of course." He reached into his suit coat, pulled out a small black leather address book and a black enameled pen. He flipped through the book, found the page he wanted, tore another page from the book's back, uncapped the pen, and wrote something on the small sheet of paper. He rose, holding the torn page out to Tom.

19

Tom stood, walked across the horse-hide rug, took the page from Carleton.

The telephone hung on the wall, a big black bakelite unit, the hand crank jutting from its right side. Tom took a step toward it and then turned back to Carleton. The lawyer had sat back down.

Tom said, "Where were you last night, Mr. Carleton?"

"Sorry, Sheriff?"

"Last night. What were you doing?"

"Recuperating."

"What from?"

Carleton smiled faintly. "The night before," he said.

"Anyone helping you out with that?"

Alonzo leaned forward. "Just a second, Sheriff. The case is closed."

"No, Peter," said Carleton. "That's all right." He turned to Tom. "Yes. Someone was. If it becomes necessary, I can provide her name."

Tom nodded, turned and walked to the telephone. He lifted the earpiece, cranked the handle.

CHAPTER FOUR

From far off, Raoul heard the sound of the telephone. As he floated up from a beautiful blankness into the grim familiar blur of exhaustion and spent bourbon, the phone's shrill ringing sounded strangely full of hope, full of promise and opportunity. It was some angel of mercy calling him, some golden guardian who wished to repair the fabric of his life, wished to return to him everything he had lost.

He fumbled his hand out from beneath the limp sodden sheet, found the receiver, croaked "Hello?"

"Mr. Raoul Whitfield?" A woman's voice.

The roof of his mouth was sticky, his parched tongue granular. His entire body was slick, oily with sweat.

"Yeah?"

"One moment, please."

Grunting, he pushed himself upright. He swung his feet to the floor and glanced around the room. In the yellow light that slanted between the slats of the venetian blinds, he saw the tossed-aside bedspread, the slumped, discarded clothing. On the end table beside him stood a pint bottle of Jim Beam, half full, its cap missing. Sunlight was spearing it, and the amber liquid inside sparkled like an evil jewel.

"Hello, New Mexico," said the woman. "Your call is through."

"Hello?" said Raoul.

"Mr. Whitfield?" A man's voice.

"Yes."

"This is Sheriff Tom Delgado in Las Vegas. I met you last year. The Fourth of July."

He sighed. "I'll take your word for it, Sheriff. What —"

"Mr. Whitfield, there's no good way to say this, but it's about Mrs. Whitfield, sir. She's dead."

"Emily?" he said stupidly. He shut his eyes, opened them again. The bottle still stood there, sparkling.

"They found her this morning, sir. I'm very sorry."

"That's impossible. Is this some kind of crazy joke?"

"No, sir. Your lawyer, Mr. Carleton, is here right now. If you want to talk to him —"

"Murray's there? Where? Where are you?"

"At Dead Horse. The ranch. You want to talk to him, Mr. Whitfield?"

"How? How did it happen?"

"They're saying suicide. We're looking into it."

"Suicide?"

"Yes, sir. You want to talk to Mr. Carleton?"

"I – what? No. I can't – Sheriff?"

"Yes, sir?"

"Tell Murray I'll call him. I need…time. I need some time."

"Yes, sir. I'll tell him."

"Thank you."

"I'm sorry, Mr. Whitfield."

"Yes. I – goodbye."

He hung up the telephone and sat there for a moment, feeling flattened. A warm droplet of sweat went fingering down through the hair of his chest.

Emily.

He reached for the bottle, lifted it, raised it to his lips, swallowed. Molten steel lurched down his throat, exploded in his stomach.

"Until the end of time, darling."

Emily, in Paris.

22

CHAPTER FIVE

Before leaving Dead Horse, Tom stopped at the bunkhouse and talked to the two ranch hands, Pablo Ramirez and Johnny Archuleta. As Alonzo had said, they claimed they had heard and seen nothing last night. Tom asked them why the Whitfields had separated, and they told him that they didn't know, but that Victor Chervet might.

He drove back to the department, made a call to the Plaza Hotel, then got the exchange on the line, talked with Monica, and had her start putting through a call to France.

• • •

Tom stepped into the hotel's restaurant, a narrow, sun-lit room lined on three sides with brick. It was nearly empty now, the white tablecloths and the silver cutlery waiting for the dinner crowd.

She was sitting over at the broad window, alone at the table, staring out at the street, out at the shady green plaza opposite the hotel.

Tom remembered Maria this morning, staring out at her new swing set. In her young face there had been longing, naked and vulnerable. This woman's face was unreadable.

She was in her early thirties, brunette, slender, attractive, and she wore a gray jacket over a gray skirt and a navy blue blouse. It was, Tom thought, probably the only dark outfit she had brought with her from New York to the bright New Mexico summer.

Holding his hat at his side, he approached her. "Miss Templeton?"

She started, turning to him with wide eyes. The skin beneath them was smudged. Her mouth looked tired.

"Sheriff Delgado?" she said.

"Yes, Ma'am. I apologize. Didn't mean to frighten you."

"No, no, sorry, I was just – Please, sit down."

He pulled out the chair across from her, sat down, placed his hat on the table.

"Would you like something?" she asked him. "Coffee?"

"No, thank you."

She leaned slightly forward. "Is it true, Sheriff? Did she really commit suicide?"

"I –"

"Because if she did, then in a way, you see, I'm partly responsible."

"My experience, Ma'am, with a suicide there's a whole lot of people feel bad about it, but usually there's only one person responsible."

She shook her head. "We had an argument a few days ago, Emily and I."

He sat back. "Argument about what, Ma'am?"

"Everything. The way she was living her life. The way she was drinking. She'd been my best friend for years, and she was drinking so much that it was painful for me to watch her. And she was taking sleeping pills every night – on top of all that liquor. I left the ranch two days ago and I got a room here."

She lowered her head. "I let her down. If I'd stayed there, at the ranch –"

"Get you folks something?" The waitress, Francy Brown, was standing to Tom's right, a small pad in one hand, a pencil in the other.

"No," said Miss Templeton. "No, thank you."

"Thanks, Francy," said Tom. "I'm fine for now."

"You want something, you just holler," she said, and turned and walked away.

He turned back to the young woman. "Okay, Ma'am," he said. "You say you left the ranch two days ago. How come you didn't just take off for New York? Why stay here?"

"My train reservations were for tomorrow. I could've changed them, but I stayed because I hoped that Emily might call me. I

24

thought that perhaps my leaving would make her...take a look at what she'd been doing to herself."

"Mrs. Whitfield, was she seeing anyone lately?"

"You mean a man, Sheriff? A lover?"

"Yeah."

"She said she was through with men. Finished with them."

"She get any strange phone calls while you were there?"

"No. Not that I'm aware of."

"Any strangers hanging around the property?"

"No."

He nodded. "And last night, Ma'am. Where were you?"

She frowned. "Here. I had dinner in the restaurant."

"Afterward?

"I went up to my room and I read for a while. I went to sleep at around ten."

He could check that with Bill Waters, the desk clerk. Waters watched the lobby like a hawk.

She said, "Why do you ask, Sheriff?"

"Just routine, Ma'am. When was it you arrived in town?"

"Two weeks ago."

"Vacation?"

She shook her head. "I knew that Emily was going through a bad time. With the divorce. I thought I could help." She shook her head. "This is all such a mess." She looked out the window. "Poor Emily."

"Mrs. Whitfield. She was unhappy about the divorce?"

She turned to him. "Of course she was. And I knew that. I should've been more sympathetic."

"She unhappy about anything else?"

"No. I don't know." She frowned. "What, for example?"

Tom moved his shoulders lightly. "What about the daughter?"

"Little Emily? What about her?"

"She wasn't around. Over in France with her father. Kind of strange, isn't it? Usually, a divorce, the mother gets custody."

"Emily loved her, Sheriff. She adored her – she talked about her all the time. Little Emily was coming out here next month, and it was the one thing Emily looked – " Suddenly her face twisted, as though she were in pain. "Who's going to tell her? Tell Emily? Who's going to tell her father?"

25

"I already did," he said. "Little while ago."

It had taken nearly an hour for the operator to get through.

"To William?" said Miss Templeton. "You talked to William? What did he say?"

"He said he understood. He said he'd tell the girl."

"That was all? He understood?"

"Yes, Ma'am."

"He's a shit," she said. She looked at him, blushed. "I'm sorry. But he truly was. A cold, self-important bastard."

Tom nodded, as though he agreed. But he knew that the friends of a divorced wife usually took her version for official.

"That why they got divorced?" he asked Miss Templeton.

She flushed slightly. "What possible difference could that make now?"

"You don't want to talk about the divorce. You were her friend; you're loyal. I understand that. But the more I know about Mrs. Whitfield, the closer I come to figuring out what happened to her."

"But if it was a suicide. . . ."

"I don't think it was, Ma'am. I think someone wanted to make it look like a suicide."

"But you said…the District Attorney thinks –"

"District Attorney thinks what he thinks. I think what I think."

"But who killed her? Who would do something like that?"

"Don't know. Why don't you tell me about that first divorce."

She turned again, looked out at the plaza. Her lower lip was caught between her teeth, as though to prevent herself from telling him anything.

"Miss Templeton," he said. "I got a daughter about the same age as Little Emily. Ten years old. Her mother died when she was two."

She turned to him. "I'm so sorry. How did it happen?"

"An accident. Doesn't matter now. Thing is, I don't like the idea of this little girl thinking her mother committed suicide when she didn't."

She looked down for a moment.

Tom waited.

Finally she looked up. "William had some evidence."

"Evidence of what?" But already he knew.

"Emily was…lonely. In her marriage, I mean. As I said, William was cold, self-absorbed. He ignored her, ignored who she was. She was an ornament, like a ring or a watch fob, something that made him look better."

Tom nodded. The wife's version again. Maybe true, maybe not.

Miss Templeton said, "And Emily is – Emily was a warm, passionate woman. She needed affection, needed to have it, needed to give it."

"She had an affair," said Tom.

Miss Templeton took a breath, sighed it out. "Yes. And of course William found out. He hired some private detectives. They obtained the evidence. If it had come out at the divorce, about the affair, Emily would've lost custody of her daughter completely."

"They made a deal. Emily and William."

"Yes. William kept custody for most of the year. Emily had three months."

Tom wondered if he could ever make such a deal. Wondered if he could give up even a single second of Maria without a fight.

As though reading his mind, Miss Templeton said, "She had no choice, Sheriff. William would've ruined her."

"No one knew about the affair?"

"A few of us did. But that's different from it being made public, in court."

He nodded.

"She was heartbroken about it – she hated to lose her daughter. But this way, at least she had Emily for part of the year."

"The affair. That wasn't with Mr. Whitfield?"

"No. She was involved with Sigourney Thayer. A poet, a playwright. She married him after the divorce from William. It was a huge mistake."

"Why?"

"She married him to justify herself, I think. She'd lost her daughter, and most of her friends knew why. She had to marry him, don't you see? If she hadn't, it would've meant that she'd have lost Emily over a tawdry little affair. Over nothing. I think she actually persuaded herself that she loved him."

27

"She didn't?"

"Well, in a way, yes, I expect she did. He was a very sweet, gentle man. She responded to that. But it wasn't enough."

"The marriage to Mr. Thayer. How long did it last?"

"A year. I think they both realized, very quickly, that it'd been a terrible idea."

"When did she meet Mr. Whitfield?"

"A few years later. Three years ago." She looked off toward the street, smiled sadly at whatever she saw out there, then turned back to him. "I've never seen her so excited. It was as though a whole new world had opened up for her. She was like a little girl."

"Where'd they meet?"

"In Paris."

CHAPTER SIX

M iss Stein was definitely a character.

A round female Buddha swathed in a long black robe, she sat immobile beside Emily on the sofa, her powerful hands resting on her broad lap. Her bristly gray hair was as short as the hair of a Roman senator, and her face, with its strong nose and thick jowls, had the same Roman gravity, inscrutable and elemental.

She was by no means attractive, not in any conventional sense, but she was certainly…impressive.

Perhaps the most impressive person in the room.

Emily glanced around, through the haze of cigarette smoke and the clatter of conversation. People were everywhere, clusters and couples, leaning toward each other in huddles of furniture, waving their hands, nodding sagely, shuffling back and forth below the framed paintings that crowded the white walls.

Most of them were types she had seen before, in New York, in Newport, here in Paris. The old roués with practiced eyes, imperceptibly scanning the room while they explained the stock market. The burly, bearded, tweedy writers who would smell, after a rain, like a wet dog. The French painters in their silly black berets and black sweaters. The young men with perfect hair and perfect clothes, attentively lighting the cigarette of the current countess. The young women, the dancers, the singers, the models, all of them hoping for something, anything, that would alter the direction they were beginning to suspect their lives were taking.

And how, really, were they any different from you, my dear?

They were younger, for one thing. They were only beginning to suspect.

She took a sip of her wine, turned back to Miss Stein, and focused on the conversation.

"So you *are* fond of James Joyce?" said Murray Carleton, who had pulled up a chair to sit alongside the arm of the sofa.

He was another type. Handsome and flamboyant in his white Byronic shirt. Slender, stylish, self-assured, black hair going elegantly gray along the temples. Extremely dishy, Jane Templeton would've said.

But there was something about his eyes – all the while he spoke and smiled and gestured, behind those eyes he was waiting and watching for something. A weakness, an opportunity.

He was a user. Not of drugs, but of people.

"Personally," said Miss Stein, "or professionally?" She spoke slowly, deliberately, as one imagined an oracle might speak.

"Professionally."

"Yes," she said. "Yes, well then, I suppose that I am fond of him. But bear in mind that he does come after me."

Carleton smiled. "Historically? Or in terms of literary significance?"

"Both," she said.

He laughed.

Smiling, Emily took another sip of wine. She glanced once again around the crowded parlor.

A miracle.

Only a moment before, he hadn't been there; and now, suddenly, he was.

He was standing halfway across the room, tall and lean and dark, a cigarette in one hand, a glass of wine in the other, his head canted slightly forward to listen to what an older man was saying. He wore a black dinner jacket, black dress slacks, a white shirt with an opened wing collar, and a black bow tie at his neck, the knot undone, the ends hanging loose. The older man's companion, a pert young blonde sheathed in fox, was staring up at this man, transfixed.

One could hardly blame her.

"Well, of course," Miss Stein was telling Carleton, "I created Hemingway."

"Excuse me," Emily said. "Miss Stein?"

30

Miss Stein turned to her, the large Roman head slowly swiveling on the thick neck. "Yes?"

"That man there. Talking to the two others. Do you know who he is?"

"Yes," she said. "As it happens, I do. He is an American named Raoul Whitfield. He was a pilot during the war and he was very brave, I am told. For two years now he has lived in the South, in Nice, and he is a writer of mystery novels, books filled with guns and dead people. They are not bad books of their kind. He is quite successful with them."

As Emily watched, Raoul Whitfield tossed back his head and laughed. It seemed to her the most genuine laugh she had ever witnessed.

Miss Stein said, "He is also quite married."

Emily turned to her. "Happily?"

"Ah well," she said. Her heavy shoulders moved in a faint Gallic shrug. "Marriage is the exchange, is it not, of one sort of freedom for another. Who can say, outside the exchange, whether the people within it are happy."

Emily sipped at her wine. "He seems…unusual."

"He is unusually handsome."

"Yes, but there's something different about him, isn't there? With most men like that, handsome men, you can sometimes sense them staring off at an invisible mirror, gauging themselves. He doesn't do that."

"We," said Miss Stein, "the onlookers, we are their mirror."

"Perhaps his mirror's been shattered," said Carleton. "Marriage will do that." He grinned. "Means seven years' bad luck."

"Marriage, you mean," said Miss Stein, "or the shattered mirror?"

"Both," he said, and smiled. He turned to Emily. "Care to meet him?"

"Do you know him?"

"Since birth," he said. He stood, held out his hand. "Come along."

She glanced at Miss Stein, who smiled enigmatically. No more oracular utterances from her; Emily was on her own.

She turned, gave her hand to Carleton, and rose from the sofa.

As he led her along the carpet, the people around her suddenly props and background, Whitfield at center stage, Carleton said, "So you're the famous Emily Thayer."

Whitfield was moving away from the couple now.

"Hardly famous," she said without looking at Carleton.

Absurd. Her heart was beating like a schoolgirl's.

"Notorious?" said Carleton.

"Possibly notorious."

"Better still. Ah, Whitfield."

The man turned, and she saw puzzlement on his face. He glanced from Carleton to her, looked back at Carleton. "Sorry," he said. "Have we met?"

"Never, old man," said Carleton, and held out his hand. "Murray Carleton."

Whitfield smiled, stuck the cigarette between his lips, shook the hand.

"And this is Emily Thayer."

He used his left hand, still holding the wine glass, to pluck the cigarette from his mouth, nipping it between his fingers, and then he offered her his right. His brown eyes were so dark that they were almost black.

She felt the warmth, the tightness along her cheeks.

Blushing? Are you really, truly blushing?

She took the hand.

"Mr. Whitfield," she said.

"Raoul," he told her.

"Emily," she said, and set free his hand. Her own was tingling.

Absurd.

"I understand, Whitfield," said Carleton, "that you're a pilot."

He smiled. "I was, yes, during the war."

"Just the man, then. Emily here is in desperate need of a quick flight around Paris."

Emily laughed, startled.

Raoul turned to her. "When?"

"Now, of course," said Carleton.

"Not necessarily now," she told Raoul.

"Nonsense," said Carleton. "The woman doesn't know her own mind. What do you say? Can you provide the flight?"

32

Raoul turned to him. "Can you provide the airplane?"

"Easiest thing in the world. You have any preference?"

"If it flies, I can fly it."

"Admirable."

"You do know," Emily said to Raoul, "that it's nearly two o'clock in the morning."

He smiled at her. "There'll be less traffic," he said.

CHAPTER SEVEN

Over the next three years, Emily would look back at this night, the salon crowded with smoke and noise, the taxi-cab to the airport, the soaring early-morning flight through the skies of Paris, and she would remember all of it as clearly as if it had happened only minutes before.

In the taxi, she and Raoul sat at opposite ends of the rear seat, strangers brought together by a single mad idea, separated for the moment by a sweep of fabric invisible in the car's dark interior.

Carleton was in the front, beside the driver. All the way out to Orly, he sat twisted around in the seat, providing an almost manic stream of chatter. It was as though he wished to keep them entertained and occupied; wished to keep them, perhaps, linked together in their folly.

"My parents," he said, "paid a fortune to send me to the best prep school in the country, which naturally kept me far away from Albuquerque. They paid a fortune to send me to the best university in the country, and the best law school in the country, both of which kept me far away from Albuquerque. Now, of course, they simply pay a fortune to keep me far away from Albuquerque."

"Pay you," she said.

"Of course."

Mixed with her own laughter, she heard Raoul's to her left, deep and loose and relaxed, sounding familiar in a way that it could not possibly be. She turned to him, but in the darkness he was merely a shadow among shadows.

"To be honest," said Carleton, "I'd be perfectly happy to stay away from Albuquerque for free." He lowered his voice. "But don't tell them that."

They laughed in the darkness, she and Raoul, together.

· · ·

It was a part of Orly she had never seen. A small corrugated metal hangar far from the main terminal, looking desolate and abandoned in the moonlight. Only a single lamp post stood at its front. In the yellow circle of light beneath it, Carleton negotiated with a young man in baggy gray overalls.

Several yards away, Emily and Raoul watched.

She turned to him. "Will this be entirely legal, Mr. Whitfield?" she asked him.

"Please," he said. "Raoul. I doubt it. Shall we retreat?"

"Do mystery writers retreat?"

In the moonlight, she could see him smile. "How did you know I was a writer?"

"Miss Stein told me. Do they?"

"Never." He smiled again. "I suspect that you're not a mystery writer, Emily."

"No," she said. "I'm not even much of a mystery, I'm afraid. But I don't retreat."

"Good."

Carleton called out to them: "Children? Come along."

They approached him. Emily glanced at Raoul.

What on earth are you doing? You're putting your life in his hands.

That, she told herself, *is exactly where I want to put it,* and she felt a rush of excitement, giddy and unsettling.

"Right," said Carleton to Raoul. "The plane's German. A Fokker, a V.38. They use it as a trainer. You can fly it?"

"Yes." He smiled. "Murray, how is it you know him?" He nodded to the young man.

"Gardeners cultivate flowers. I cultivate people. One never knows who might be helpful, down the road. As it happens, Armand here has been very helpful." He slapped the young man on the back, and the young man grinned at Raoul.

"The plane has radios," said Carleton, "so you'll be able to talk to each other. The tanks are full, oil and gas. You can have it until tomorrow afternoon. The owner will be back in Paris tomorrow night. When you return the plane, you pay Armand for the fuel you've used. You have money with you?"

"Yes."

"Well, then. Have a lovely flight." He held out his hand.

Raoul took it. "I'm at the Ritz until Thursday. Let's have a drink before I go."

"Done," said Carleton. He plucked a white card from his shirt pocket, handed it to Raoul. "Call me."

He turned to Emily, held out his hand again. She gave him hers, and he bent over it, kissed it, released it. "Bon voyage," he said.

· · ·

It was a bi-plane, two wings and two open cockpits.

Raoul leaned from his cockpit toward hers and adjusted her headset and her microphone. He was only a silhouette in the light of the moon, but when the backs of his fingers brushed lightly against her cheek, the touch lingered on her skin as though painted there.

He turned around and seated himself, slipped on his own head set, flicked some switches on the instrument panel.

She heard his voice in her earphones, thin and tinny, "Can you hear me?"

"Yes," she said.

She wondered if he could somehow hear the beating of her pulse, thumping now against the phones. She had been on airplanes before, but never a bi-plane. Never a bi-plane at night, flown by a man she barely knew.

All that, surely, would explain the beating of her pulse.

"You're ready?" he asked.

"Yes."

He gave a thumbs-up signal to Armand, and the young man reached up and grabbed the propeller, tested the tension, paused for a moment, then jerked it quickly down and nimbly stepped back.

36

The engine caught immediately, and she felt its vibration in the narrow leather seat beneath her and along the thin soles of her shoes. Raoul had borrowed a pair of goggles and a pair of battered leather flight jackets from Armand, and now she pulled her jacket tightly against her chest and zippered it up. It smelled of hair tonic and of sour, goaty perspiration.

She didn't care.

Raoul taxied down the length of the runway, then slowly wheeled the plane around, into the wind. The roar of the engine and the tremor of the plane's fuselage increased for a few moments, and so did the beat of her pulse. The plane lurched once and began moving forward, lumbering down the runway, then racing along it; and then, smoothly, effortlessly, impossibly, they were in the air.

• • •

It was absolutely spectacular.

All of Paris was spread out beneath them, a gift given in a dream: the tiny streets, the glittering black ribbon of the Seine, the hunched cathedral of Notre Dame, a few firefly lights of automobiles creeping along the Champs Elysees. To her right, the brightly lit Eiffel Tower rose up like a Christmas tree from the spangled darkness. Above the tower, and above them, the full moon shared their sky.

The wind swept against her cheeks; her hair snapped against her neck.

"Are you still buckled in?" she heard him say.

"Yes."

"Want to try something?"

"Everything!" she said.

The roar of the engine grew louder and the nose of the plane rose. They went skyward at an increasing angle, and then they were vertical, and then – No! – they swung slowly upside down, Paris abruptly over her head, gravity swelling her face, and she squealed like a school girl, and then they came swooping, slowly, deliciously slowly, around to level flight, and the world was righted once more.

She laughed, elated. "Again," she called into the microphone. "Please?"

And again Raoul flew the plane up, up, up, until it was aiming directly for heaven, and then he laid it over in a long, slow, graceful loop.

Again, helplessly, she laughed.

Raoul came over the microphone: "Would Madame care for some wine?"

"But we didn't bring any."

"What would Madame prefer?"

"I think, oh, I think a Burgundy."

"Burgundy it is."

• • •

A warm, bright summer morning, the sky blue, the air still, a few delirious birds chirping away in the forest to their right.

They sat on their flight jackets in the field, their picnic spread out on the old blanket Raoul had bought when he bought the food: cheese, bread, some salty green olives, two tomatoes, pâté, two bottles of red wine.

She raised her glass, a simple kitchen glass half-filled, and she examined the wine. "Burgundy for breakfast," she said. She smiled at him. "In Burgundy."

"Wine's got more kick in the morning." His voice became professorially serious — nasal and precise. "Much more economical to drink it then, don't you know."

She laughed. "It wasn't terribly economical, what you paid the farmer for all this."

The flight had been marvelous. In the moonlight they had sailed southeast from Paris, followed the winding black Seine for a time, miniature silver farms and vineyards slipping by beneath them, and then they had struck due south, floating over the small brown city of Auxerre just as the stars above were fading off into the pale pink sky. Raoul had flown on until he spotted the farmhouse and the empty field, and then he had brought down the plane, flawlessly. A few jolly bumps along the stubbled ground, a wobble or two of the wings, a long luxurious stretch for the two of them after they clambered from the cockpits, and then an early morning haggle with the startled farmer and his wary wife.

Raoul tore a piece from the baguette. "Sometimes," he said in his professor's voice, "in order to save money, one must spend it." He cut a slice of cheese with his jackknife, slipped it onto the bread. "More?"

"Please," she said.

He handed it to her, and she watched as he sliced some cheese for himself.

She took another sip of wine, set down the glass. "It must be lovely to be a writer," she said.

He looked over at her. "Why?"

"You make magic little marks on a blank sheet of paper, and you create whole worlds, don't you? And you put people into the worlds, imaginary people, and then other people – real people, us, the readers – we live with them for a while."

He smiled. "Well, yes. But it does takes a certain amount of work."

"But art always takes a certain amount work, doesn't it? A certain amount of bravery."

Another smile. "Those are big words, Emily. Art. Bravery. I write mystery novels."

"Yes, but you still come face-to-face, everyday, with a blank sheet of paper."

"Yes."

"And you create worlds there. And that's still magic, isn't it?"

"For me, it is," he said simply.

"And you love it."

"I hate it."

"Liar."

"Yes, I do. I love it. God help me."

"And it's like flying, too, in a way. It's a kind of freedom. It lets you go wherever you like."

His smile was wry. "If you sell the books."

"Miss Stein said you were very successful." She took a final bite of the bread and cheese.

"Moderately successful. I've got a roof over my head."

She swallowed. "Yes, in Nice, for two years now. Nice is nice. What's your wife's name?"

"Is there anything Miss Stein didn't tell you?"

"She didn't tell me your wife's name."

"Prudence."

"Prudence? Honestly?"

"Cross my heart."

"And is she?"

"Prudent? Very."

She smiled, waved a hand at the blanket and the food. "It's obviously not contagious."

"Perhaps not. Sadly."

"How long have you been married?"

"Ten years."

She nodded. "The pâté is good, isn't it?"

"Very good."

"Are you in love?"

"With the pâté?"

"Mr. Whitfield is stalling."

"We know each other, Prudence and I."

"Is that as good, knowing someone, as loving them?"

"In my experience, it's more dependable. What about you? Married?"

"Twice, but not now. Now I'm just a flighty divorcee. Taking moonlit flights."

He smiled. "Children?"

"One. A daughter. She lives most of the year with her father. And you?"

"No."

"Does it bother you?"

"What?"

"My having a daughter."

"Why should it bother me?"

"No reason. It bothers some men. She's a wonderful girl."

"That doesn't surprise me."

She smiled. "A compliment?"

He held up his glass. "The wine talking."

She laughed. She lifted the bottle, poured herself some more.

Her heart was beating again now; and she knew, by its pace, that it was time.

A door stands closed before you, ornately decorated, adorned

40

with beaten gold and hammered silver. Beyond it lies a mystery. Bliss, rapture, disillusion, grief — who could know?

Do you open the door and take that single irrevocable step inside it, or do you simply turn from it and walk away? And never learn what lies beyond.

She raised her glass but didn't drink from it. "I like you, Raoul," she said. "And I'd like to know you. Would you like to know me?"

He sipped at his wine. "I think that might be a very dangerous thing."

"You told Mr. Carleton you're leaving Paris on Thursday."

He peered into his glass, studying the wine, then looked over to her. "That's right."

"Less than a week away. We haven't much time then, have we?"

He looked at her for a moment longer, and then he set down his glass and moved toward her. She felt herself open up to him, all her flesh alive, trembling like a flower.

41

CHAPTER EIGHT

Tom Delgado nodded to Miss Templeton.

"A pretty story, Ma'am. They steal a plane—"

"They didn't steal it. They paid for the fuel."

"Owner was probably real grateful."

"Sheriff, it was a lark. The plane wasn't hurt. No one was hurt."

"Mr. Whitfield – wasn't he married at the time?"

She looked down. They had both ordered coffee, and finished it, and now she adjusted the empty cup in its saucer, turning it slightly to the right. "Yes," she said. She looked up. "And you're right, of course. I'm sure she was hurt. Raoul left her a week after he went back to Nice. He and Emily were married when his divorce became final."

"In Paris?"

"In New York. The both went there after he left his wife. They were there for a year, until the divorce became final."

"You were in Paris when she met him?"

"New York. She told me about it afterward." She took a deep breath. "As I said, she was like a little girl. She was so happy." Her face tightened and she shook her head as though to rid herself of some painful thought.

"What, Ma'am?" he said.

"I keep thinking that if I'd stayed out there, at the ranch, then none of this would've happened."

"We think that way, sometimes, because it makes us feel like we got control over things. But usually it's not true."

"But if someone wanted to kill her, Sheriff, and I was out there, he wouldn't have gone ahead with it, would he?"

42

"Or maybe you'd be dead, too."

Skeptical: "Two suicides?"

"One murder, one suicide. Distraught wife kills friend, then self."

She frowned and then looked off, out the window. She nodded sadly. "So I'm alive now because I left, and Emily isn't."

"She didn't die because you left, Ma'am. She died because someone killed her."

She didn't respond.

"What brought the two of them out here?" he asked her. "Raoul and Emily."

"Murray Carleton."

He frowned.

She turned to him. "You don't like him," she said.

He smiled. "He's a lawyer. I'm a little prejudiced."

"I don't much care for him either. There's something about him that…I don't know. He's…Machiavellian. D'you know what I mean?"

He smiled again. "I read a book once."

"Of course. I'm sorry, Sheriff."

"Forget it."

"I must sound like an ass."

"Not a bit of it. You go ahead, Ma'am. Murray Carleton."

"Yes. Well, he inherited some money and he moved out here."

He nodded. "Couple years ago."

"Yes, and he came to their wedding, Raoul and Emily's, in New York, and he invited them out here for their honeymoon. They fell in love with the place. The countryside, the light, the history. Mr. Carleton helped them buy the ranch."

"Whose money bought it?"

"What do you mean?"

"Emily's or Raoul's?"

"I don't know who actually paid for it, but they both had money. Emily had more, of course, but Raoul had money from his books. He was doing very well."

"Seen his books around," said Tom. "Not lately, though."

"I don't know why that is. I can't speak for him. But I can tell

43

you, Sheriff, that he was no gigolo." Abruptly she frowned at him. "You don't think he was involved in Emily's death?"

"Don't think anything yet, Ma'am. But nobody broke into that house. Both doors were locked. And Mrs. Whitfield is dead. Murdered, I think. Means someone with access, one way or another. What we need is a motive. You know if Mrs. Whitfield had a will?"

She shook her head. "No, Sheriff. Raoul would never hurt Emily. Never."

He nodded. "She have a will?"

"She made one right after they got married. They both did, she and Raoul, and they both left everything to each other."

"Who hired the foreman? Mr. Chervet?"

"Raoul did. But he wouldn't hurt her either."

"He's the only other person in the house."

"He took care of her. He was dedicated to her."

"Dedicated how?"

"He's a decent man, loyal and honest. He's a good man. He liked Emily. He respected her."

"Nothing between them, you could see?"

"Romantic? Absolutely not."

"You were only there for a few days, Miss Templeton."

"I would've seen something. Noticed something."

He nodded. "Mrs. Whitfield – she ever tell you why she separated from her husband?"

"She refused to talk about it. But Mr. Chervet was there. He may know."

Again, Tom nodded.

Time to talk to Mr. Chervet.

CHAPTER NINE

Slouched against his seat, Raoul stared out at the bleak, blinding landscape. His shirt was soaked. Even with the window drawn down, with all the windows in the entire Pullman car drawn down, the air inside was suffocating. The breeze that blundered in, baked between the sun and sand of the Mojave, was oven-hot, sucking away life like a vampire.

Another hour to Barstow.

How long to Dead Horse?

A lifetime.

• • •

Those first few days in Paris, they went everywhere together. Lunch at Le Dôme and Le Procope, drinks at Le Café de la Paix and Le Flore and Les Deux Magots, dinner at La Tour d'Argent and Fouquet's. Hand in hand they strolled along the cobblestones of the Ile St. Louis, along the paths of the Luxembourg Gardens, through the cemetery of Montmartre, through the cool green shade of the Bois de Boulogne.

And then at night, in her hotel or his, they came together, flesh against flesh, Emily's sleek supple body beneath his, or beside it, or astride it, her fingers clutching at him, her head thrown back, her mouth awry, her slender throat taut with cries of strangled, desperate, ecstasy.

But it hadn't been only the love-making. It had been Emily herself, her awesome presence, Emily walking beside him, sitting across from him, her blue eyes so beautiful and so open that he could not look into them, into her, without feeling the claw of pain along his chest.

Occasionally he thought of Nice, of home and Prudence. But these impossible moments spent with Emily Thayer were a kind of time out of time, and he knew that when they ended, they would be gone forever, as if they had never happened, and his life would continue as it had before. As uneventful, as familiar.

They spent that Wednesday night at a tiny bistro on the Left Bank, dark, dim, nearly deserted, those blue eyes as shiny in the candlelight as jewels at the bottom of a stream.

Over the coffee and brandy, she took a deep breath. "So," she said. "Our last night together."

"I hate the idea."

"I hate it like poison. But I'm being very grown up about it, don't you think?"

"More than I am, probably."

"It would be lovely, wouldn't it, if we were both absolutely free? If we could go anywhere we liked, do anything we liked?"

"Yes," he said, and for the first time he felt a flicker of shame.

Surprisingly, it was shame not for his betrayal of Prudence, but for his betrayal of Emily. His past, his present, his dull middle-class existence – they had all become a burden now; for her and abruptly, because of her, for him.

Freedom, yes. He wished that he had it, so he might offer it to her.

And then he realized that the wish was a worse betrayal of Prudence, of their marriage, than all the hours he had spent with the woman sitting across from him.

He took a sip of brandy.

"It would be wonderful," she said. "We could live wherever we wanted – Morocco or Tahiti or the south of Spain."

"Somewhere sunny."

"Somewhere sunny, yes. And you could write your books and I could bring tea and crumpets into the study." She smiled happily. "And we could have lovely dinner parties, all of our friends, and whenever we liked, we could take off for somewhere else – for Paris or New York or Istanbul."

Feeling empty behind his smile, he said, "It would mean writing quite a lot of books."

46

"Oh, but darling, I've got money, tons of it, and what good is it if you can't spend it with someone you...care about?"

He looked down at the table, at the hand that held his brandy glass.

Immediately she reached over and put her hand over his. "I'm sorry, darling. I'm being silly. I promised myself I wouldn't talk like this. I'm spoiling things, and I don't want to."

He rolled his hand over, clasped her fingers with his. "I —"

"*There* you are."

Raoul turned and saw Murray Carleton, in a long black opera cloak, sailing toward them through the shadows of the restaurant.

Raoul slipped his hand out from beneath Emily's. And felt, once again, that he had betrayed her, through simple cowardice this time, a craven fear of exposure.

"How'd you find us?" he asked Carleton. He tried to keep the irritation from his voice.

"The concierge at the Ritz. Never let the concierge make your reservations."

"Murray, it's the last night that Mrs. Thayer and I —"

"I know, old man, and that's why I forgive you. For not calling me about that drink you mentioned. I understand perfectly."

Carleton's card lay in Raoul's wallet, unread. Emily's presence had intervened.

"Yes," he said, "I'm sorry, but —"

"Not to worry," said Carleton. He turned to Emily. "You look lovely tonight, my dear."

She smiled faintly. "Thank you. But you know, Mr. Carleton, this is the last —"

Carleton held up his hand. "I know, I know. That's why you're getting the present."

"What present?" said Raoul.

"Can't tell you. Have to show you. I promise it'll take only an hour. Come on, children. I'd really like to do something for you both."

He looked back and forth between them, and then smiled. "You won't always be this young, you know. You won't always have the freedom you have now."

Freedom, thought Raoul. He looked at Emily.

47

She smiled at him, turned the smile to Carleton, and held up her index finger. "One hour," she said. "No more."

"*Absolument,*" he said.

• • •

It was a bordello. An elegant bordello, red velvet curtains and Persian carpets and darkly gleaming mahogany walls; but a bordello nonetheless, and Raoul wondered what Carleton had been thinking.

But Emily, of course, handled it all beautifully. As the liveried butler led them through the sitting room, through the scents of perfume and powder, through the sound of jazz piano tinkling from the gramophone, she merely looked with mild curiosity at the women sitting there, two of them in floral dressing gowns, the other two in black silk lingerie, black silk stockings, black high-heeled shoes. The women ignored them, nattering to each other about a hair dresser on the Place Vendôme.

Raoul, Emily, and Carleton followed the man down a narrow corridor, the walls lined with flocked red paper. He came to a door, nodded to Carleton, to Emily and Raoul, and then went padding away.

Carleton opened the door, stepped in. "Come along, children."

It was a large, lavish boudoir, softly lit by electric lights set behind frosted glass sconces. Against one wall was a big four poster bed, a white satin duvet draped across the thick mattress, plump white satin pillows gathered at its head. Against the opposite wall lay a black velvet divan embroidered in gold. Before the divan crouched a long, ornately carved teakwood table. To the table's right stood a silver champagne stand, a bottle of Cristal nestled in the silver bucket. Atop the table, neatly organized, were three empty champagne flutes, a blue-flamed alcohol lamp, a small rectangular brass box and a small brass cylinder holding splinters of bamboo, and a thin spidery object with a tiny enameled bowl and a gently arched ivory stem. Raoul recognized it as an opium pipe.

"Sit, sit," said Carleton, and gestured toward the divan. As they moved toward it, he knelt down beside the table.

Emily and Raoul sat. "What on earth are you doing?" Emily asked him.

"Getting your present ready."

"Hashish?" she said.

"Opium," said Raoul.

She turned to him. "You've smoked it?" She sounded intrigued.

"Once," he told her.

"Safe as mother's milk," said Carleton, rolling a small black bead of opium between his fingers. He placed it in the bowl of the pipe, handed the pipe to Raoul, lifted a sliver of bamboo from the cylinder, held it to the flickering flame of the lamp until it flared, then leaned forward, offering it to Raoul.

Raoul glanced at Emily, who was leaning slightly forward, attentive, a smile on her lips, her blue eyes watching him.

He inhaled, felt the smoke flow harsh at the back of his throat, felt it seep deep into his lungs. Almost immediately a sweet lassitude spilled out from his center, out along his joints and muscles.

He handed the pipe to Emily. She looked at him, placed the pipe's ivory bit in her mouth, inhaled, held the smoke for a moment, and then slowly exhaled. She sat back, staring off across the room, and then she blinked several times. She turned to him, radiantly smiling. "It's really quite lovely, isn't it?"

He grinned at her.

Carleton stood, took off his cloak, hooked his finger over the collar, swung the cloak back over his shoulder, and looked down at them silently, as though waiting for something.

Raoul smiled up at him, and said, "Thank you, Murray. This is all very generous. Thank you."

Carleton's expression didn't change. His glance flicked to Emily, back to Raoul. For another moment he stood there, and then, curtly, coldly, he said, "Don't mention it." He turned, the cloak swinging out from him like a cape, and he stalked across the room, tugged open the door, and slipped out, slamming the door behind him.

Raoul looked at Emily. "What was that about?"

Her eyes were sparkling. "I think Murray wanted to join us, darling."

"Smoking opium?"

"Is it possible for a mystery writer to be so naïve?"

He glanced at the door, and suddenly he understood. He turned back to her. "Ah," he said.

"Ah." She handed him the pipe.

Holding it, he glanced down at the table. "Three glasses. Not two." He turned to her. "I hadn't realized that Murray was interested in you."

She smiled again. "Not only in me."

He frowned.

"Ah," he repeated.

"Maybe you should consider writing cook books, darling."

"Maybe I should." He inhaled on the pipe. "Poor Murray," he said, exhaling.

"Poor us. Wednesday night and Thursday half-way here."

In the gentle light she looked more beautiful than he had ever seen her.

"There's something I want to say," he told her.

She put her hand on his arm. "Maybe you shouldn't, Raoul. Maybe neither of us should say anything."

"It's just this. No matter what happens, tomorrow, next year, I'll never forget this past week."

She moved her hand to the side of his face, her palm cool and soft along his cheek. "Neither will I," she said. "Until the end of time, darling."

• • •

The next day he left for Nice. A week later, exhausted, exhilarated, he left Nice and Prudence, and he returned to Paris and Emily.

At the Gare de Lyon, they found each other beneath that enormous spiderweb ceiling of glass and iron. Holding his face in both hands now, she looked up at him. Her blue eyes were liquid, glittering. "Is it true, darling? We can be together?"

"For as long as you'll have me."

Her hands tightened against his cheeks. Fiercely, she said, "Until the end of time."

CHAPTER TEN

For the second time that day, Tom knocked on the Dead Horse front door.

In the west, the sun was sliding down the sky.

The door was opened by a thin, short, wiry man, maybe forty years old, wearing jeans and a workshirt faded to pale blue. His skin was as dark as a field hand's; his features were a mixture of Spanish and Asiatic.

"Mr. Chervet?" said Tom.

"Yes, sir."

"I'm Sheriff Delgado. Mind if I come in?"

"No, sir. Come in, sir."

• • •

"You didn't hear the gunshot at all?" Tom asked.

"No, sir. The radio was on."

They were sitting at opposite sides of the kitchen table, Tom's heavy forearms resting on the polished maplewood, Chervet leaning back in his chair, his thin arms crossed over his chest.

Tom said, "Your room's less than twenty feet away, Mr. Chervet."

"Yes, sir. But I am a heavy sleeper. Once I am asleep, I stay asleep. Always, I am like this. And the walls of the house, they are very thick."

"How come you were sleeping inside the house and not down at the bunkhouse?"

"Mrs. Whitfield, she asks me to move into one of the guest

51

rooms. After Mr. Whitfield leaves. She is nervous to sleep in the house alone."

"What time did you go to sleep last night?"

"After twelve. Ten minutes. Maybe fifteen minutes."

"And when did Mrs. Whitfield go to bed?"

"Sir, I tell you this already."

Tom nodded. "Trying to get it straight in my head. What time?"

"Eleven o'clock."

"That bottle of pills, Luminal, on the table right next to her bed. She take one of those?"

"I do not know, sir. I think so. I think she takes one every night."

"How long's she been taking them for?"

"The pills, sir? Since March. Since after Mr. Whitfield leaves."

Tom nodded. "And when she went to bed, the doors were already locked?"

"Yes, sir. At ten. Always I lock them at ten. The front and the back"

"Okay. Tell me about this morning."

"I come in to light the fire. In to her room."

"You knock on the door first?"

"Yes. There is no answer. But very often Mrs. Whitfield is still asleep when I come in."

"You do that every day?"

"Yes, sir. Every day when the mornings are cold. And when I go in today, I see her there. On the bed."

"Where was the pistol?"

"In her hand."

"Right hand or left?"

"Her right hand."

"She was right-handed."

"Yes, sir."

"You recognized the pistol."

Chervet nodded. "Mrs. Whitfield's gun."

"Why'd she need a pistol?"

"She is nervous, as I tell you. Out here in the country, so far from the town."

"But you were always here, right? Only a few feet away."

"Yes, sir. But with the gun, Mrs. Whitfield, she feels more safe."

"Where's the pistol now?"

"The District Attorney. Mr. Alonzo. He takes it."

Tom sat back, pulled his Colt from its holster, opened the cylinder, held his hand beneath it as he tapped the ejector rod. The cartridges tumbled into his palm. He set them on the table, closed the cylinder, handed the weapon to Chervet. "Show me how she was holding it," he said.

Chervet held the pistol as though he had never handled one before. Awkwardly, he reversed it, so the barrel was pointed toward his chest, and then he wrapped his right fingers around the back of the grip and slipped his thumb through the trigger guard.

"Like this," he said. "And her hand, it is out on the bed, like this." He held the weapon away from him.

Tom nodded and reached for the pistol. Chervet handed it to him.

Again, Tom opened the cylinder. He slipped one of the cartridges into a chamber. "Why'd you take it out of her hand, Mr. Chervet?"

"I tell them, sir. The coroner's jury. I think maybe I can do something for Mrs. Whitfield."

Tom slipped in another cartridge. "Like what?"

"Sir, I don't know. I am confused."

Tom finished loading the pistol, slid it back into the holster.

Chervet was shaking his head. "It was so bad, sir, so horrible to see her lying like that. She is so still. And the blood." He looked off.

"Was Mrs. Whitfield seeing anybody else?"

Chervet was still staring off into the past.

"Mr. Chervet?"

He turned back to Tom. "Sir?"

"After Mr. Whitfield left, did Mrs. Whitfield see any other men?"

"Oh, no, sir. She stays in the house; she never comes into the town."

"No men came out there?"

"No, sir."

"How long you known Mr. Whitfield?"

He turned back to Tom, blinked, lifted his chin. "For many years, sir. I know him in the Philippines."

"How?"

"My family, they have a farm, sir. On Mindanao, the big island. And his family, they have a farm close to us. I know him as a child."

"When did you come to the States?"

"Five years ago. In 1930. I come to New York, sir, to find work, and Mr. Whitfield, he helps me."

"What kind of work?"

"In the construction, sir. Building things."

"You got any experience running a ranch?"

"Not a ranch, sir, but a farm. On the island, before I leave, I run my family's farm."

"Even so, how come he didn't he hire someone local?"

"Mr. Whitfield, he visits with me when he comes back to New York."

"Two years ago."

"Yes, sir. He sees I am not happy with the construction work. With the life of the city. Then he marries Mrs. Whitfield and he comes out here. And then he sends me a letter and he asks me if I want to work here with him. To run the ranch for him. I say, sure."

"You still have the letter?"

"No, sir. It was only a letter."

"How were they getting along then, Mr. Chervet?"

"They love each other, sir. They are crazy for each other."

CHAPTER ELEVEN

Raoul and Victor watched the two bulldozers scrape away at the stubborn yellow earth. The ground here in New Mexico was like rock. And the air was parched, bone dry even in the fall – when the rain did come, it disappeared at once, sucked deep into the sand and stone.

The big machines growled, moaned, whined. White smoke puffed from their chimney-like exhaust pipes and stuttered up into the clear blue sky.

"It's got to be perfectly level," said Raoul. "Before the topsoil and the grass go in. We don't want the horses stumbling all over each other, like Keystone Kops."

He was shirtless, his skin nearly as brown now as Victor's, as brown as it had been when he was a boy, decades ago on Mindanao. On his head he wore a straw hat, cowboy style. A red cowboy bandana was knotted at his neck.

"No, of course," said Victor. He smiled. "But polo?"

Raoul grinned. "The first polo field in New Mexico." He clapped Victor on the back. "We're pioneers, man!"

"Yes, but who are you playing with?"

"Lots of rich people in town, Victor, people from back east. We'll give 'em something to do besides count the silverware." He grinned again. "And if that doesn't work, then we'll find some cowboys and Indians, and we'll teach them how to play."

They heard a horn blare in the distance and they turned to see Mrs. Whitfield's big Cadillac come sweeping down the dirt road from the main house, a cloud of dust tumbling behind it.

The car braked, tires spitting up more dust, and the door opened and Mrs. Whitfield glided out, as beautiful as ever in a bright, lemon yellow dress. She shut the door and turned to her husband, smiling happily. "You look gorgeous, darling. How can a man be so flamboyant in just jeans and boots and a handkerchief?"

"Madame forgets the chapeau," he said, and he tipped his hat gracefully forward.

She laughed, went up to him and wrapped her arms around him, leaning her body against the length of his. They kissed. Her left hand, white against the brown skin, slid smoothly down the arc of his back. His fingers pressed beneath the blade of her shoulders.

Victor, made suddenly invisible, glanced off at the construction crew.

Mrs. Whitfield pulled herself lightly away from Raoul and she turned to him and smiled. "Hello, Victor."

He bobbed his head. "Mrs. Whitfield." As always in her presence – the beauty, the elegance – he felt clumsy and somehow irrelevant.

One arm still around her, Raoul waved his hat at the field. "Look at it, Em. They're almost done. We start putting down the topsoil tomorrow."

"That's wonderful, darling. You're not going to chop down the piñon, are you?"

Standing alongside the field, it was a big tree, probably the tallest piñon on the ranch.

"Nope. We'll put the bleachers right next to it. In the shade."

"Good."

"We'll be playing by next March."

"I'm very happy for you. Truly I am."

"You're sure you don't want me to find you a horse?"

"No. Thank you ever so much, but no. You handle the equestrian affairs, darling, and I'll tend to the house. Speaking of which – I've something to show you. A surprise. Victor? Do you mind if I borrow my husband for a few minutes?"

"No, Ma'am. Of course not."

"What surprise?" said Raoul.

"If I told you, it wouldn't be a surprise."

"Let me get my shirt."

"You won't need it, darling. This won't take long."

• • •

An hour and a half later, as Victor was talking to one of the bulldozer drivers, Raoul drove back in the Cadillac. He was alone.

He got out of the car, lifted his shirt from the ground, shook it, swiped it across his shiny forehead, shook it again, and then put it on. Buttoning it up, he came toward Victor. His hair was matted.

He smiled. "You knew all about it," he said.

"Some of it, yes," said Victor. "Johnny and Pablo, they help her the most."

Raoul laughed. "You bastard," he said, and punched him lightly on the shoulder. "Have you seen it?"

"No. She believes if I see it, I think, I will tell you."

"You've got to see it. Come on."

• • •

A hundred yards from the main house, tucked in between the piñons and junipers, was a small adobe building, freshly painted in pale brown. Raoul stopped the Cadillac before it, opened the car's door, and got out. Victor stepped out the passenger side.

Raoul walked up the path, opened the building's front door, and stood back. "Go ahead," he said. "Take a look."

Victor walked into the building. The air smelled of paint and cut lumber.

There were bookshelves packed with shiny books. There were expensive carpets on the floor and framed paintings on the walls. There was a brand new roll-top desk, a brand new typewriter sitting atop it, beside a neat white stack of typing paper. There were two plump, comfortable-looking chairs and, against one wall, a long matching sofa.

Behind him, Raoul said, "She got most of this in Santa Fe."

"Yes, I know."

"Bastard," said Raoul.

Victor smiled.

"It's great, though, isn't it?" said Raoul, looking around.

57

"It is very beautiful. She works very hard for you."

"I'll say."

He walked over to a bookcase, ran his fingers along the backs of the books. Then he moved over to the desk, reached out and touched the typewriter with the tips of his fingers. "Victor?" he said without looking back.

"Yes, sir?"

"Do you remember where I put my old typewriter? The Royal?"

"In the hallway closet. But Mrs. Whitfield, she asks me to get rid of it."

Raoul turned to him.

"On Monday," said Victor. "She says she bought you a new one, and she tells me not to say anything. It is a part of the surprise, she says. I give the old one to Pablo, and he takes it into town, with the trash."

For a moment, Raoul said nothing. Then he grinned again. "Good. I always hated the damn thing."

CHAPTER TWELVE

An hour more until Flagstaff.
Dark outside now, moonless. Occasionally, off in the distance, he could see a single light glimmering in the murk, a star fallen to earth. A ranch house, probably, or an isolated cabin. Someone out there in the endless night, sharing warmth and safety with someone else, with his wife, his family.

During the train's long slow climb into the mountains, the interior of the Pullman had grown cooler. Like the other passengers, Raoul had closed his window.

Now he pulled up his coat's collar, drew the coat more tightly about him, crossed his arms over his chest, tucked his hands beneath them.

It had gone so wrong, the thing between him and Emily.

And it had been, in the beginning, such a miracle.

All the people in the world, bustling helplessly about, wounded and crippled and lost, dimly seeking some kind of perfection: and he and Emily, against the odds, had found it in each other.

They had been so happy together. He remembered the day she had shown him the study.

• • •

She had driven him up to it in the Cadillac.

"You're done with the guest house?" he asked her.

"It's not exactly a guest house," she said. "That was a tiny little fib, I'm afraid. I'm sorry, darling, but I didn't want you to know until it was finished."

"What was finished?"

59

"Come on."

They got out of the car and walked up to the adobe building. At the front door, she reached with both hands to her neck, drew a thin gold chain up over her head. Dangling from it was a house key. "Here," she said, and held it out to him

He took the key, closed his fist around it. "Still warm," he said, and raised his eyebrows, leering.

She pushed him toward the front door. "Go. Look."

He unlocked the door and stepped in. He felt her move behind him, following.

It was spectacular. A bright airy room, high ceilings, lace curtains at the windows. Persian carpets on the bleached hardwood floor. A polished desk, a shining typewriter. Leather furniture – huge padded chairs, an enormous sofa. Leather-bound books everywhere, hundreds of them. Paintings – impressionist landscapes and still lifes, a Georgia O'Keeffe poppy, red and lush, aswirl with sensuality.

He turned to her.

"I ordered the books in Santa Fe," she said. "The Encyclopedia Britannica. The Oxford English Dictionary. It's huge, darling – twenty volumes – but the man at the store said it was the very best."

He grinned. "It is."

He wandered up to one of the bookcases, ran his fingers down the leather spine of a book. Roget's Thesaurus.

"It's all fantastic, Em."

He walked to the desk, looked down at the typewriter.

"I had to go to Albuquerque for that," she said. "It's a Remington. It's supposed to be very good."

"It is," he said, turning to her. "It's the very best, Em. And so are you."

"Do you really like it, darling? The studio, I mean. Tell the truth."

Raoul walked over to her, placed his hands on her shoulders, looked down into her face. Looking up at him, she rested her forearms along his chest, her palms flat against his skin.

"I love it," he said. "It's perfect. Thank you."

"If you don't like anything, you can change it. Just throw it out. Burn it, if you want. I mean that, darling – I won't mind, I promise. It's your studio. It should be exactly the way you want it to be."

"It's perfect now."

"I'm so pleased you like it."

He looked around the room. "You did all this by yourself?"

"Well...Johnny and Pablo did help with the big things."

"It's absolutely perfect, Em." He beamed down at her. "You know what? I'm going to come over here tonight. I'm going to start the first chapter of that new book. I've been thinking –"

"Oh, no, darling, not tonight. Remember? The Lorillards and the Grants are coming down from town."

"Tomorrow, then," he said. "And you'll be bringing me tea and crumpets?"

"On a silver platter." Her fingers kneaded his chest. "But right now I should check with Estella about the food."

"You can't go yet."

"Why not?"

"We need to inspect the sofa."

She smiled. "Inspect it how?"

He slid his hand down and cupped her breast. Her eyes shut and her lips parted, and he bent down to her.

• • •

"We'll need something to drape over the sofa," she said. "A blanket. Some kind of throw."

They lay next to each, naked.

He smiled. "The leather's a bit slippery, isn't it?"

He was on his back, one arm behind his head, the other curled around her shoulder. She was on her side, propped on her left elbow, her breasts soft along his ribcage. Their clothes were scattered across the floor.

"It can't be wool, though," she said. "Wool scratches."

He shut his eyes. "We don't want that."

"But you do like it?" she said. "The sofa?"

His eyes still shut, he smiled again. "Even more so now."

She ran the tip of her index finger down his forehead, along his nose, over his mouth and chin, tracing the line of his profile.

61

Laying her hand on his chest, she said, "Do you think we'll always be this happy, darling?"

"Hmm," he said. "Haven't you asked me that question before?"

"I'm asking again."

Eyes still shut, he said in his professor's voice, "I can see no reason to believe otherwise, Mrs. Whitfield."

"But you were happy with Prudence."

"Different kind of happiness."

"Different how?"

"More a friendship than a marriage."

"Were you ever unfaithful to her?"

"You know I was."

"I mean before me."

"There were a couple of incidents. They didn't mean anything."

"How could they not mean anything?"

He opened his eyes, turned to her. "They weren't important, Em. They were momentary things."

"Did Prudence know?"

"Yes."

"How could she bear it?"

"I told you. She was a friend. We were together for ten years, Em."

"Do you still think about her?"

"Sometimes. I think about most of the people I've known."

"Do you miss her?"

He smiled. "I'm too busy rolling around on sofas with you."

"But you spent so much time with her. So much of your life."

"My life has changed."

"You have to promise me something, darling."

"What?"

"You know what."

"No other women?"

"Yes."

He smiled. "I promise."

"I mean it, darling. I simply couldn't bear it. It would ruin everything."

"It's an easy promise to make."

"All promises are easy to make."

"It's an easy promise to keep."

"You're a gorgeous man, darling, and women are attracted to you like flies to honey."

In his professor's voice, he announced, "Flies, I believe, are more attracted to shit."

She smiled. "Then don't be a shit."

Grinning, he stroked her hair. "I love you, Em. I want us to stay together. For ten years, twenty years."

"What happens after twenty years?"

"We renegotiate?"

She slapped his chest. He laughed.

She rose up onto her elbow. "I should go," she said. "The food. Dinner."

"Are you sure?" He rolled onto his side, facing her, and slid his left hand down over her breast, over her belly, down between her legs.

"Umm," she said, and closed her eyes. "Delicious. I love it when you touch me there."

"So do I," he said.

"Oh," she said. "Yes. Do that."

CHAPTER THIRTEEN

The train began to pull away from the Flagstaff station. Along the platform, departed passengers slowly wandered, dazed by travel. The light that fell from the lamps was bleak and isolating, like the light in an Edward Hopper painting.

He sat back.

It had been so good.

They had sometimes argued, yes. She had sometimes misunderstood. Sometimes, she had disagreed with him. She had disliked Murray Carleton.

"He's like one of those lizards," she said, "who change their color to match the background. In Paris, he was a rich bohemian. Here he's a rich cowboy."

They were in bed, Emily in a black silk slip under the sheet, Raoul naked beside her.

"A chameleon," he said. "What's wrong with a chameleon?"

"It doesn't have any true color. It exists only against a background. Like Murray. He's hollow inside."

He smiled. "According to the best scientific evidence, chameleons aren't hollow."

"Murray is, I think. And I'll never forget the way he looked at us in Paris, that last night. When we didn't ask him to stay with us. He was furious."

"Maybe we misinterpreted –"

"I didn't misinterpret, darling."

"He brought us out here. He put us up for weeks. If it hadn't been for him, we wouldn't have Dead Horse."

"Then we'd have something else. But we'd still be together. Isn't that the important thing?"

64

"You aren't happy here?"

"Oh, darling, of course I am. Ecstatically happy. But I'd be happy anywhere, so long as you were with me."

"Ecstatically?"

"Ecstatically."

"Have I mentioned that I love you?"

"Not recently."

"I love you."

"I love you too. But I don't love Murray Carleton."

"I accept that. You don't even have to like Murray Carleton."

"Good. Because I doubt I ever will."

So, yes, from time to time they had disagreed. People disagree, in any marriage, any relationship. People are different, one from the other. But the disagreements, the differences, had merely made the love they shared seem firmer and more substantial, so tightly woven that it was impregnable.

And then, slowly, it had begun to unravel.

If he could pick out one moment, one single incident, when the threads began to snap away, what would it be?

That first big party. The polo party.

Everyone had come. Dash Hammett from California. Murray, all their friends from town.

• • •

The clomp of hoofbeats all around, the ground racing by below.

His pony swerved beneath him, its hindquarters pumping. On his right, forty yards away, Dale Bradley, his second man, was spurring his own pony toward the ball and raising his mallet. Already, Eddie Shortbent of the Gold Team was galloping for the goal posts, to block the shot he knew Raoul would try.

The score was tied, the fourth and final chukker, less than a minute left in the game.

Bradley's mallet clapped against the ball and the ball soared, bounced, then rocketed over the grass toward Raoul. Bradley spun the pony around and raced toward Shortbent, trying to cut him off at the goal.

Raoul clamped his heels against Diamond's flanks, rose in the stirrups, leaned forward, and lifted the mallet.

The ball skittered along the field. He focused on it, centered his entire being on it. And then, ferociously, he swung, and he felt a solid smack against the head of the mallet. He jerked on the reins and wheeled Diamond to the left.

Shortbent nearly made it. His pony's hooves dug into the grass, hurling up clots of dirt, and Shortbent pushed himself from the stirrups and raised his mallet.

But the ball shot past him, a yard ahead, and went ripping along the ground and across the line, just inside the left post.

Game over.

Distantly, Raoul heard people screaming, applauding.

He looked toward the big piñon, the bleachers.

Where was Em?

There, amid the others, waving at him frantically from beneath the white canopy.

Laughing, triumphant, he stood in the stirrups and waved the mallet over his head.

• • •

A clutch of guests milled along the bar, beneath the other canopy. People slapped him on the shoulder, called out "Terrific shot!" He grinned and nodded, grinned and shook hands. Victor gave him a towel and a cold, sweating glass of bourbon and ice, and Raoul blotted at his face, swung the towel up onto his shoulder, took a long, cool, swallow of Old Fitzgerald.

Dash Hammett loomed up, lean and saturnine, his eyes amused beneath that shock of white hair, a glass in his hand. He wore the inevitable white business shirt and black slacks.

"Very impressive," he said.

"You should try it sometime," Raoul told him.

"Horses and I have an understanding. They don't ride me and I don't ride them."

"Gets the blood racing."

"I don't want my blood doing anything that I won't do."

"Raoul?"

He turned.

66

Young Sandra Cooper, visiting for the summer at the next ranch, up the road toward town. Maybe nineteen years old, brunette, pretty in a college-girl way, unformed and eager.

"That was wonderful," she said.

"Glad you liked it."

He introduced the girl to Dash. After smiling a quick hello, she turned back to Raoul.

"And you rode beautifully," she said. "It must give you an amazing sense of freedom to ride like that. It must be lovely to have all that strength and…power between your legs."

Taking a sip of his bourbon, he glanced at Dash, who was raising his own glass to hide a smile behind it.

"It has its moments," he told the girl.

"Few and far between as they are," said Dash.

She turned to him.

"For me personally," he said. He smiled. "For Raoul, obviously, they happen all the time."

She looked back at Raoul. "I've never ridden, myself. I've always wanted to learn."

Dash took another sip, his eyes amused over the rim of his glass.

"You should," Raoul told her. "Plenty of horses around. It won't take you long."

She said, "I wonder –"

"Darling!"

Emily, her face alight. "You were spectacular!"

He laughed. "It went pretty well, didn't it?"

"It went superbly." She kissed him and then turned to Sandra, her eyebrows raised inquisitively.

The girl's face was flushed and she was blinking. Unformed. Not really ready for grown ups.

"Em," said Raoul, "this is Sandra Cooper. She's staying with the Kearnses for the summer."

Emily smiled. "Hello, Sandra," she said sweetly.

The girl blinked again. "Hello, Mrs. Whitfield. I'm very pleased to meet you."

Dash glanced at Raoul and Emily and Sandra, then held up his glass. "Out of gas. Time to refuel." He slipped away.

Her voice still sweet, Emily said to Sandra, "And how do you like New Mexico?"

"I just love it. It's all so incredibly beautiful, isn't it?"

Raoul said, "Sandra wants to learn how to ride."

"Oh, you must," Emily told the girl, and then seemed puzzled. "But don't the Kearnses have horses?"

"Yes, they do, but, well, you know, I hate to impose on them like that. I —"

"Who's imposing upon whom?" said Murray Carleton, who had come up behind Emily, a drink in his hand. His black hair tousled, his face shining, he looked trim and athletic in his polo clothes – a white short-sleeved shirt, brown whipcord trousers, a pair of glistening black boots.

Emily smiled at him politely. "Murray, have you met Sandra Cooper?"

"I have now," he said, beaming at the girl. "Murray Carleton. Charmed."

"How do you do," she said.

"Sandra," said Emily, "was just saying that she'd like to learn how to ride."

"Well, then," he told the girl, "you must find yourself a teacher of impeccable credentials. I recommend…," he frowned, thoughtful, and then beamed at her again, "…myself."

Sandra smiled uncertainly. "Thank you, but —"

"No thank yous, no buts. Come along. I'll introduce you to my horse."

Taking her by the elbow, he steered her out toward the field. She looked back over her shoulder, at Raoul and Emily. Emily waved at her, cheerfully.

Raoul grinned. "Not very nice, Em. Murray will chew her up and spit her out."

"She deserves it. I saw the way she was looking at you, the little minx."

He laughed. "Little minx?"

She leaned toward him, slid her arm around his waist, looked up at him. "Do you miss those days, darling?"

"Which days?"

"The days of chewing them up and spitting them out. The days when you were free."

"No," he said, and put his arm along her shoulder. "I couldn't be happier."

"But you're not writing, darling."

"I told you, Em. I needed a break. I was writing every single day for ten years."

"Sometimes I think that your not writing…that it's a way to punish me."

He dropped his arm. "Punish you? For what?"

"I don't know. For not making you happy?"

"But you do make me happy."

Her arm fell from his waist. Her face had changed: subtly, the planes and curves had grown harder. "You wrote when you were with Prudence."

"I didn't have any choice."

"You said you loved it. Writing."

"I did. I do."

"How do you know, if you don't do it?"

"It's just a break, Em."

"Maybe I'm not good for you."

"That's crazy."

"Maybe you'd be happier with someone like Sandra."

"For God's sake. She's twelve years old."

"She's eighteen years old, going on thirty-five."

"Come on, Em. You can't keep getting upset every time some girl talks to me. When a man gets accused of cheating, again and again, he starts thinking that maybe he should just go ahead and cheat."

She narrowed her eyes. "Is that a threat?"

"We're not really talking about Sandra, are we? We're talking about Prudence. You've got some idea that –"

"No, we're talking about us."

"Em, look, if you don't trust me, then what's the point of our being together?"

"Exactly," she said.

"Oh, come on."

"I have to go to the house," she said coolly, and turned and walked away.

CHAPTER FOURTEEN

Tom looked across the kitchen table and said, "They were getting along fine at the beginning. When you first came out here."

"Yes, sir," said Chervet. "They are in love with each other, very much."

"What happened? Later?"

Chervet looked down.

"Mr. Chervet, all I'm looking for is the truth. You understand?"

Still staring at the floor, the man nodded.

"Mrs. Whitfield is dead, and I want to find out why. You liked her?"

Chervet looked up. "Oh yes, sir. Very much. She is a good woman."

"Then help me here."

Chervet took a breath. "Mrs. Whitfield, she is…she is also a jealous woman, sometimes."

Tom nodded.

"And Mr. Whitfield," said Chervet, "he is a handsome man. The women, they all like him. Even when he is young, this happens. In the Philippines."

"And here?"

"Sometimes they have arguments. Mr. and Mrs. Whitfield."

"About women?"

"Yes. Sometimes, yes. She accuses him, you know? And he says she is wrong. But always, you know, they make up. They go back to loving each other."

"Was there one argument in particular? One woman in particular?"

Chervet frowned.

"Mr. Chervet?"

He nodded. "One day she comes to me. Mrs. Whitfield. She asks me to drive her into the town."

"Thought she knew how to drive."

"Her vision, in the night it is not good. At night, she does not see. And this is in the evening. It is almost dark."

Tom nodded. "Go ahead."

CHAPTER FIFTEEN

Victor was in the courtyard, talking to Pablo. One of the house cats had disappeared overnight, probably snatched by a coyote, and Victor wanted to put out some poison. Pablo, who had worked on ranches for over forty years, said that coyotes could eat a ton of poison, two tons of it, and it would only make them stronger and smarter. But Pablo had spent those forty years learning how to find reasons for not doing anything.

It was February and the air was cold. Snow had fallen the week before, but the sun had burned it from the courtyard except in the shadow of the encircling adobe wall, where it lay in gray, crusted shelves.

The front door flew open and Mrs. Whitfield slammed the door behind her and rushed across the portal, fumbling at the buttons of her long wool coat. Her purse was slung over her left shoulder and she held a slip of paper in her right hand.

"Victor!" she said.

"Yes, Ma'am?"

"I need you to drive me. Into town."

"Now, Mrs. Whitfield?"

"Yes, now, dammit!"

He swung away, his face burning, and he moved toward the gate.

"Victor?"

He turned back.

She stood there, her head lowered, her left hand raised to her forehead, thumb and fingers clamped against her temples. She dropped her hand, raised her head. "I'm sorry. I'm very sorry. But please. Get the car."

"Yes, Ma'am."

72

• • •

It was a long, silent drive. Mrs. Whitfield sat on the far end of the seat, her purse on her lap, her left hand clenched atop it. Her right elbow was propped on the door's arm rest, her chin notched into her opened hand. With her hair hiding her face, she stared out the window toward the ridges and valleys in the east.

Or maybe, thought Victor, she was staring out beyond the ridges, out beyond New Mexico, out across the width of the continent, all the way back to the distant East Coast, where she had been raised. Sometimes at the ranch, when Victor looked off at the dry jumbled countryside to the west, he imagined the deserts of Arizona and California, and then the bright blue endless sprawl of the Pacific, and then the loamy green fields and lush green jungles of home.

Once, about halfway to town, he tried to talk to her. "Mrs. Whitfield —"

"No, Victor." She turned to him. "Please."

He nodded, and she turned back to the window.

They left 66 at Romeroville, where the highway swung south, and they continued north along the narrow black state road, winding through the hills and along the arroyos. The sun had set now and the shadows of things had disappeared. A grayness was settling.

When they were two or three miles from Las Vegas, Victor turned to her. "Where in the town, Mrs. Whitfield?"

She sat up, opened her left hand. The piece of paper was there, crumpled now. She opened it, flattened it against her purse, held it toward the diminishing light from the window. "Rincon Street." She lowered the paper to her purse, covered it with both hands. "It's off Armijo."

"I take Grand Street?"

"Yes," she said, staring straight ahead now, her body rigid. "Yes."

When they got there, he saw that it was an older neighborhood, small cramped houses on tiny lots. There were no streetlights, no sidewalks.

73

Stiffly, Mrs. Whitfield opened her purse, searched through it, found a box of matches. She lit one, held it to the piece of paper. Her hand shook. The flame wavered. "Number 112. It must be in this block. There. Stop the car."

He braked, pulled the car over to the right, stopped it.

It was another small house, gray in the darkness. There were no lights on, inside or out.

"No one is home, Mrs. Whitfield."

She was looking at the house. "You stay in the car, please, Victor."

"No, Ma'am. This neighborhood is no good. I come with you."

She turned to him, her lips pursed. But she must have understood that neither of them had a choice. She nodded.

They got out of the car, shut their doors. He waited for her to come around the rear of the Cadillac, then followed her up a pathway worn into the spare, stubbled grass. They climbed some creaking narrow steps to a small, roofed porch. Mrs. Whitfield pulled open the screen, rapped her knuckles against the wooden door.

Nothing happened.

Whatever this was going to be, Victor knew it wouldn't be good.

"No one is home, Ma'am," he told her.

Leaning forward, her head cocked toward the door, she held up a silencing hand. Then she rapped at the door again, louder this time.

A light snapped on, over their heads, and the door opened.

A small thin woman stood behind the screen, very young, using one small fist to hold a trench coat closed over her front. Beneath it she wore a black nightgown. Her hair was short and black, as shiny as the fur of a cat. Her face, too, was cat-like – narrow cheeks, broad cheekbones, and large brown eyes shaped like almonds.

She looked from Mrs. Whitfield to Victor, back to Mrs. Whitfield.

"What?" she said.

"I want my husband."

"You want a husband, lady, write to Miss Lonelyhearts."

74

"I know he's here."

"Nobody here but me and the cockroaches."

Mrs. Whitfield ripped open the screen, pushed her aside, stalked into the house. The screen slammed shut and the woman shouted, "Hey!" She spun around and followed.

Victor hesitated. Go in or stay out?

Stay out, unless she needed him. Unless someone needed him.

This was not a thing he wanted to see.

Through the screen he heard Mrs. Whitfield coldly say, "I knew you were here."

"Emily —" Raoul's voice.

Sighing, Victor leaned against the wall of the house and put his head back along the cold wood.

"You bastard," said Mrs. Whitfield.

"Look, there's no reason —"

"You bastard!"

"Emily —"

Victor flinched at the sound of a slap, loud and sharp and final.

"Hey!" said the young woman.

Mrs. Whitfield shouted, "You've been cheating on me the whole time. From the beginning."

"Goddamit, that's not true. I look at another woman and you're all over me. I'm a goddamn prisoner."

Victor closed his eyes.

Her voice rose. "You want your freedom? Take it! You want this piece of trash? Take her! You come to the ranch tomorrow and you get your things. All of them. I won't be there. I'll be in Santa Fe, talking to a lawyer."

"Emily. Listen to me —"

"You made your bed. And hers. Now you lie in it. You won't ever lie in mine again."

"Emily," he called, but she came bursting through the front door, smacking the screen open with both hands. Victor watched her as she dashed down the steps, staggered, nearly fell, then righted herself and tottered across the lawn, toward the car.

He began to follow her.

"Victor," he heard behind him.

Reluctantly, he turned.

It was Raoul at the doorway now, holding the screen open, a towel wrapped across his waist .

Victor felt a stab of shame. Not at Raoul's nakedness, but at the expression on his face. Even as a child, he had never looked so lost and frightened.

"Victor," he said. "Talk to her. Please."

Under the porch light, Victor could see the clownish red blotch on the side of his face, where Mrs. Whitfield had struck him.

Victor looked away from it, nodding hopelessly. "I try."

"Please, Victor."

"Yes." He turned and trudged down the steps, across the lawn, opened the Cadillac's door and got in. Mrs. Whitfield sat over at the far end again, her head bowed, her arms crossed.

He started the car, drove it out into the street.

"Lois," she said flatly.

"Excuse me, Ma'am?"

She cleared her throat. "Lois Bell. That's her name."

Lowering her head still farther, she tightened her arms against her stomach, as though she wanted to prevent herself from spinning apart. And then slowly, her breath catching in her throat, she began to sob.

CHAPTER SIXTEEN

L ois Bell," said Tom. "You sure you got the name right?"
"Yes, sir," said Chervet. "Lois Bell."
"On Rincon Street?"
"Yes, sir."
"How'd Mrs. Whitfield know to go there?"
"I do not know. Someone called her, sir, on the telephone?"
"You don't know who."
"No, sir."
"What happened then?"
"The next day, sir, she goes to Santa Fe. He comes here, Mr. Whitfield, and he takes some clothes away."
"He say where he was staying?"
"That Plaza Hotel, sir."
"When did she get back from Santa Fe?"
"After a week. After he leaves for California."
"The two of them ever talk together?"
"No, sir. He calls here every day, before he leaves. I talk to him. He wants me to talk to her."
"You do that?"
"Yes, sir. On the telephone, when she is in Santa Fe. And after, when she comes back. But she is proud."
"Mr. Whitfield ever call from California?"
"Yes, sir. He tries. But she does not take the phone call."
"Mrs. Whitfield ever talk to —"
Someone knocked at the front door.
"Excuse me, sir," said Chervet. He got up and walked toward the entranceway.
Tom looked at his watch. Eight o'clock. He would be busy for a

77

couple more hours. He needed to call Mrs. Gomez soon, talk to Maria, apologize, tell her he couldn't pick her up tonight. He'd get her in the morning.

Murray Carleton stepped into the room, smiling, followed by Chervet.

"Sheriff," Carleton said. "What a surprise. I thought the case was closed. Isn't that what the District Attorney said?"

"Just filling in a few holes."

"Holes," said Carleton. He leaned back against a counter, crossed his arms. "Very enterprising of you."

"And what're you doing here, Mr. Carleton?"

"Not that it's any of your business, but I wanted to make sure that everything was ready for Raoul."

"When's he getting back?"

"Tomorrow."

"What time?"

Carleton frowned. "You're not thinking about interrogating him, I hope."

"Interrogating, no. Talking to him, yeah."

"Sheriff, the man's wife is dead."

"That'd be why I want to talk to him."

"As his lawyer, I can't let you interview him unless I'm present."

Tom stood. "Fine. You set it up. Give me a call."

As he moved toward the door, Carleton said, "Sheriff, does Peter Alonzo know you're out here, badgering Mr. Chervet?"

Tom stopped. Chervet had been standing off to one side, holding onto his thin upper left arm with his right hand as he watched them. Tom asked him, "Mr. Chervet, I been badgering you?"

"No, sir." He turned to Carleton. "The Sheriff, Mr. Carleton, he is only asking questions."

Carleton turned to Tom. "One definition of badgering."

"Not mine," said Tom.

"Maybe I should have a little talk with Peter."

Tom smiled. "You sure you want to do that, Mr. Carleton? Threaten me?"

"No one's threatening anyone, Sheriff."

"Glad to hear it. Oh. Before I forget. You told me that Mrs. Whitfield was unhappy because she missed her daughter."

"I told you that was one of the reasons she was unhappy."

"Funny, though. I heard the daughter was coming out here soon."

"Emily was depressed about the divorce. Depressed people don't necessarily think rationally. I believe you know that."

Tom looked at him.

"I made some inquiries," said Carleton. "I learned about your wife. Her suicide."

With an effort, Tom kept his voice flat. "It was an accident."

"That's what the coroner's jury ruled. But everyone in town —"

"Everyone in town is wrong."

"Is that likely?"

"About this, yeah."

Carleton uncrossed his arms, put his hands along the edge of the counter. "Sheriff, listen to me. I'm not your enemy. And I do sympathize. However it happened, you lost your wife, and your daughter lost her mother. And now Emily's daughter has lost a mother. I can understand why you might be taking all this a bit personally."

"What I take personally," said Tom, "is murder."

"But this wasn't murder, Sheriff. Emily was distraught. She killed herself."

Tom nodded. "You said you were with someone last night, Mr. Carleton. Who was that?"

Carleton sighed. "A friend," he said.

"Friend got a name?"

"Lois Bell. The barmaid at the Cantina."

Tom glanced at Chervet, saw that he was staring at the lawyer.

"What time?" Tom asked Carleton.

"I went to the bar at midnight. We left at one and went to my house. We were there all night. Until this morning, when I got that call from Mr. Chervet here. Satisfied?"

"I heard that Mr. Whitfield and Lois Bell were involved."

Smiling, Carleton crossed his arms again. "If you know Miss Bell, Sheriff, then you know that she's not exactly monogamous."

Tom nodded. "Also heard that Mrs. Whitfield found her husband at Lois Bell's house one night."

"Raoul told me. It was foolish of him – seeing Miss Bell, I mean. Jeopardizing his marriage. But it was the first time he'd ever done anything like that."

"This morning you said they'd just drifted apart."

"If they hadn't, would Raoul be spending time with Miss Bell?"

"Don't remember you mentioning Miss Bell."

"Raoul is my client, Sheriff. Confidentiality."

"Right. So how do you figure Mrs. Whitfield knew he'd be there?"

"I haven't the faintest idea."

"You never asked Lois Bell?"

Carleton smiled. "The question never came up."

Tom nodded. "Right. Thank you."

"My pleasure, Sheriff."

CHAPTER SEVENTEEN

Tom walked into the Cantina at a little after nine. As always, the bar smelled of old beer and old cigarettes.

It was early yet and business was slow. A couple of railroad workmen sat at one end of the bar, a shot glass and a beer bottle in front of each. At a table in one dim corner, Jesse Parker from the Esso station sat alone and glared at a glass of beer. The Santiago brothers, leaning toward each other over another table, sat back when they saw Tom. Behind the bar, Lois Bell stood polishing a highball glass. She wore a tight red silk blouse, open at the neck, and a black cotton broomstick skirt. The color of her lipstick matched the color of the blouse.

She glanced at Tom, looked down again at the glass.

He sat down on the stool in front of her. She looked up and said, "What'll it be, Tom?"

"Cup of coffee, please."

"It's not fresh-made."

He smiled. "There's a shock."

"Just letting you know."

"Appreciate it, Lois."

"Cream? Sugar?"

"No thanks."

She put the glass, upside down, beside a row of identical glasses on the back bar, then sauntered over to the coffee urn, the skirt swaying at her calves. She held a cup under the spigot, filled it, grabbed a saucer, slipped it under the cup, walked back up the bar and set them both in front of Tom.

"Thanks," he said.

She picked up another glass, began to polish it.

He said, "What've you gotten into now, Lois?"

She looked up. "How's that, Tom?"

He took a sip of coffee. "What is it with you? You been a heartbreak to your parents since you were twelve."

"Yeah. Weird. What with them being so good to me and all."

"I know Ed. I know he's tough —"

"No, you don't," she said. "Believe me, Tom, you don't know Ed."

He left that alone. "Maybe so, but —"

"And besides, there was a time when none of that bothered you any. One time, anyway. A Tuesday night, if I remember right. Last year."

He nodded. "We already covered that ground, Lois. It's not something I'm real proud of."

"Yeah. You said."

It had been the anniversary of Carla's death. Maria had been with Mrs. Gomez. Loneliness and self-pity had driven him to the bar that Tuesday, and somehow, at the end of the night, in a kind of blur, he had found himself with Lois in her tiny house on Rincon Street. What bothered him afterward wasn't what they'd done together. What bothered him was letting himself feel so bad that he'd wanted to forget who he was, and then letting himself use Lois to do that.

"Water under the bridge," he said.

"Sure."

"When was it you got involved with Raoul Whitfield?"

"Who said I was involved?"

"Mrs. Whitfield found him at your place. Back in February."

She shrugged, turned, set the glass beside the others, turned back, picked up a fresh one.

"He was a married man, Lois."

She glanced up from the glass, smiled. "Not married to me."

"That's kind of the point."

She polished the glass.

"You know she's dead," he said.

"I heard. Too bad."

"All choked up about it, I guess."

"I only met her once." She looked up, smiled sourly. "We didn't get along."

"Where were you last night?"

"You already know where I was."

Tom nodded. "Carleton called you, told you I was coming."

"You're a mind-reader, Tom."

"Interesting."

"What?"

"I talk to Carleton. He tells me he was with you. Before I get here, he calls and tells you what to say."

"If he really told me what to say, you think I'd let you know he called?"

He smiled. "Never said you were stupid, Lois. You knew I could ask at the exchange, find out if anyone from Dead Horse called here tonight."

"He called because he didn't want you blindsiding me."

"Considerate."

She turned to the two workmen at the end of the bar. "José? Who did I leave here with last night?"

The man glanced at Tom. "Nobody," he said.

"No," she said. "Tell the truth."

"Murray Carleton," he said.

"What time?" she said.

"Closing. Around one."

She looked at Tom.

He nodded. "Uh huh. Now I'm convinced."

Again, Lois shrugged. She wiped at the glass.

Tom took another sip of coffee. "That glass about clean yet?"

She put down the glass, tossed the towel beside it, leaned against the back bar, and crossed her arms. "What do you want, Tom?"

"Where'd you meet Whitfield?"

"Here."

"When?"

"Like you said. In February."

"Tell me about it."

CHAPTER EIGHTEEN

It was late and Lois was tired. Tired and bored. Pouring booze into deadbeat boozers wasn't the most thrilling way to live your life.

And Sundays were always dead. Most of the regulars had spent all their weekend money, and all their weekend energy, by closing time on Saturday.

She looked at the clock. It was set fifteen minutes fast, but it still said only twelve o'clock. Old Enfield, the owner, didn't want her giving last call until a quarter to one. She could get around that, she could always get around Enfield, but usually it wasn't worth the trouble.

It wasn't worth the trouble tonight. Like the customers, she didn't have anywhere else to go.

She picked up a shot glass, flipped it over, lifted the bottle of Chivas, filled the glass, replaced the bottle. Turning around to face the room, leaning against the back bar, she took a sip.

The place was nearly empty. A couple of old farmers at one end of the bar, Esteban Morales and his cousin. At the other end, a couple of drag-ass railroad workers. And over in the corner of the room, old Jesse Parker, the owner of the Esso Station. Jesse had a mortgage on that corner table.

Not a single Prince Charming in the bunch.

Later, and often, she would remember that thought.

As she took another sip, the front door swung open and Murray Carleton toppled in, his arm on the shoulder of another man, both of them doubled over with laughter.

Things were looking up.

84

Murray had a house up on Eighth Street, a fabulous place, all towers and pinnacles and big bay windows. Gorgeous furniture inside, the best booze, the best food, the newest jazz records, cool silk sheets on a bed the size of a swimming pool. Okay, he was kind of twisted, a back-door man, maybe even a little fruity, but he was funny in a dark, nasty way that always made her laugh. And he was generous.

She'd seen the other man around. Slim and sleek, as tall as Murray but even better looking. She'd asked about him, learned he had a rich wife and a ranch south of town, which put him out of her league. Theoretically, anyway.

What was he doing with Murray? Maybe he was a little fruity himself?

The two had stopped laughing now, and they moved toward her with the stiff, precise walk that men used when they were hiding the big fat secret that they were bombed.

She set her glass of Scotch on the back bar.

"Ah, Lois!" said Murray. He held his arms out at his sides. "She walks in beauty, like the night!"

"You been into the cooking sherry again, Murray," she said. She glanced at the other man. He was smiling at her.

"Not a single dram," Murray said. "Lois, I want you to meet a very good friend of mine, from days of yore. This is Raoul Whitfield. Raoul, this is the lovely Lois Bell."

"Hello, Lois," the man said. He wore a long white silk scarf that hung outside the collar of his black topcoat, something Lois had never understood. How the hell does it keep you warm if it's on the outside?

"H'lo," she said.

"Raoul is a poet, Lois, a bard. A purveyor of words and wisdom."

She turned to Raoul. "There any money in that?"

He laughed. "Occasionally," he said. "Murray, what would you like?"

"A long and wicked life," he announced. "And marriage to a rich widow with a bad cough."

Raoul smiled. "Like to drink," he said.

"I do indeed," said Murray. "In fact, I believe I'll have a small

85

Scotch and soda. But you children give me a moment while I repair to the gentlemen's room."

"You find any gentlemen in there," said Lois, "you let me know."

Murray chuckled and shuffled off.

"What'll you have?" she asked Raoul.

"The same, please." He sat down on a stool.

She could feel him watching her as she made the drinks: a faint, pleasant pressure along the surface of her skin. She knew she moved well, her hands fast and nimble. But when she set the glasses on the bar, one for him and one for Murray, he only smiled politely and said "Thank you."

The side of the beer cooler poked out from beneath the bar, forming a small ledge under it. She sat on the cooler, rested her right forearm along the bartop. "Raoul," she said. "That's like a French name."

"Yes."

"But you're not French."

"No."

"You're a writer."

"Occasionally."

"Published and all?"

"Yes."

"It must be nice. Being a writer."

He glanced down at his drink for a moment. When he looked up, his face was blank. "Do you think so?"

She shrugged. "You get to live where you want to. How you want to."

"Occasionally," he said. He took a big sip of Scotch and soda.

"You own that big ranch, south of town. Dead Horse."

"No," he said. "My wife owns that big ranch, south of town."

"There's a difference?"

He thought it over. At last he said, "Occasionally."

"You like that word a lot. You ever use any others? And don't say 'occasionally'."

"Sometimes," he said.

She laughed.

He smiled and said, "May I buy you a drink, Miss Bell?"

86

She turned, lifted the shotglass from the back counter, held it up. "Got one already. And the name is Lois. What'll we drink to?"

He raised his glass. "To freedom."

"Sounds good to me." She clinked her glass against his.

They each drank.

He said, "How long have you lived here, Lois?"

"Here in town? Too long."

"Where would you like to be?"

"Just about anywhere else." She looked at him levelly. "What about you, Raoul. Where would you like to be?"

Again he seemed to be thinking over an answer, but then he frowned and turned left, turned right. "Where's Murray?" he said.

"No idea. Maybe he passed out in the can."

"Has he ever done that?"

"No." She smiled. "But Murray's full of surprises."

"I'd better check on him."

"Over there. That hallway. First door on the right."

He swung the stool around, stood up, swayed very slightly for an instant, and then set off across the room. She watched him, then tossed back the rest of her Chivas.

Behind her, at the far end of the bar, Esteban Morales called out to her: "This one's married, Chiquita."

Lois nodded, then turned to him. "That's not always a character flaw, Esteban."

"You gonna get in trouble."

"So what else is new?"

Esteban cackled, and then shut up and turned away when he saw Raoul returning.

Raoul looked worried. "The door's locked and he won't answer. He's still in there."

Lois stood. "Shit," she said.

She crossed the rubber padding to the bar's entrance, swung up the panel, headed across the room for the hallway. Raoul followed.

At the men's room door, she reached into her pocket, pulled out her keys. She stuck one in the lock, turned it, pushed open the door, and stepped in.

Sitting on the closed toilet with his arms folded and his head nestled against the sidewall, Murray Carleton was sound asleep.

Gently, she prodded his shoulder.

Mumbling something, Murray sluggishly shook his head. He didn't open his eyes.

She prodded him again, less gently. "Hey. Murray! The bar's on fire."

"G'way," he said.

"Swell," she said.

Raoul was standing beside her. Behind the smell of Scotch, there was a faint scent of aftershave or cologne, something expensive. "What now?" he asked her.

She turned to him, looked up at his face, saw that his eyes were very dark, almost black. Exactly like hers.

He stepped slightly back, away from her, as though the room had suddenly grown too small. Maybe he'd seen the same thing.

She felt a small flicker of something. Satisfaction?

"What time is it?" she asked him.

He glanced at a gold wristwatch. "A little after twelve."

"You got a car?"

"Just outside."

Screw Enfield, she thought.

"I was closing up anyway," she told him. "I'll help you get him home. But I'll need a ride to my place afterward. Okay?"

"Of course. Thank you. I appreciate the help."

"Part of the job," she said.

• • •

Raoul waited in the office while she chased everyone out. Old Esteban was the last to leave, giving her a wink as he wobbled out the door. When she punched him on the shoulder, he cackled.

There wasn't much cleaning up to do – she hadn't done enough business to get anything dirty. She counted the till, counted her bank for tomorrow, stuffed the money into the safe. By twenty after twelve, she and Raoul were helping Murray out to Raoul's car, a big Lincoln sedan. They dumped him in the back seat, Murray grumbling at them, and then Raoul held open the passenger door for her. She liked that.

They didn't talk about much – the weather, the new restaurants in town, where to go in Santa Fe for a decent drink. But her ribs were a bit tight around her lungs, and when she laughed, she could hear herself. The laughter sounded forced to her, tinny, and she wondered how it sounded to him.

By the time they got to Murray's place, Murray had sobered up some, but it was still a piece of slapstick getting him out of that back seat and up the wide steps that led to his front door. Finally, they managed it. On the porch, Murray found his keys and then let himself in, calling out over his shoulder, "Adios, compadres!" He slammed the door shut.

Raoul turned to her. "Thanks again."

"Like I said. Part of the job."

"Come on," he said. "I'll get you home."

When they returned to the car, he held open the door for her.

● ● ●

They spoke even less on the way to her house. The air inside the Lincoln seemed to become denser. She could still smell his cologne.

She gave him directions and he followed them. Within only a few minutes they were on Rincon Street, and he was pulling up in front of her house.

For a second or two, they both sat there. Then he said, "It was good to meet you, Lois."

"You too," she said. Her porch light was on, and some of the glow spilled over her shoulder into the car. She could just make out his features. "Want to come in for a drink?"

He smiled. "Thanks. But I've had enough for tonight."

"Coffee? A glass of water?"

He said nothing..

"I won't bite," she told him.

He nodded. "I could use a glass of water."

"Come on then."

"I'll get the door for you."

She waited, watching him through the windshield as he walked around the front of the car. He opened the door, held out his hand. She took it, and it was warm and strong. She slid from the seat of the Lincoln and the hand left hers. All at once hers felt exposed and abandoned.

He followed her across the yard, up the steps. She unlocked the door and turned on the light, and he followed her in.

"It's not much," she said. "But it's mine. Mine and the bank's."

His hands in his topcoat pockets now, Raoul looked around the room.

She tried to see it with his eyes. The beige walls, the small sofa, the coffee table, the two small chairs. The Navajo carpet. The Georgia O'Keeffe print. Everything neat and tidy.

It would all fit, probably, inside one of his bathrooms.

He smiled. "It's very nice," he told her.

"Yeah, but it's cold," she said. "I'll start the fire – it's all set to go. And then I'll get your water."

This afternoon, before going to work, she had arranged the crumbled newspaper, the kindling, the split cedar logs in the kiva fireplace. Now she took a match from the metal container on the floor, struck it against the interior wall of the fireplace, lit the newspaper, tossed the match between the logs.

He was watching her, his face empty. She said, "Be right back." Smiling, he nodded.

She went into the kitchen, unbuttoned her coat, took it off and slung it over the chair. She smoothed the front of her skirt, arranged the collar of her blouse, made sure the second button was undone, and then took a glass from the cabinet, filled it at the faucet. When she returned to the living room, he still stood there with his hands in his pockets. He was staring at the print on the wall.

"Georgia O'Keeffe," she said. "I think it's sexy. You like her stuff?"

He turned to her. "My wife does. I have the same painting in my study. My office."

She handed him the glass. "Then I guess we got the same good taste. Me and your wife."

He swallowed some water. "So it seems."

"Let me take your coat," she said.

"I should go."

90

She nodded slowly, looking at him. "She keeps you on a tight leash."

He surprised her by smiling. "How old are you?"

"Nineteen. What difference does it make?"

He laughed softly.

"What's so damn funny?"

"That's a question that only makes sense when you're nineteen." He smiled again. "And what would you know about leashes?"

"I been on one all my life. My father. This diddly-squat town." She frowned. "I don't like being laughed at."

"I wasn't laughing at you, Lois."

"At what then?"

He sipped at his water. "At myself, probably."

"I don't like that either."

"Why not?"

"You shouldn't do it. You're too good for that."

"You've known me for a total of − what? One hour?"

"I been around bars since I was sixteen. I know people. I know men."

Another smile. "What do you know about me, Lois?"

"I know you're unhappy."

He looked at her.

She reached forward, took the glass, stepped over to the coffee table, put it down, stepped back to him.

"I should go," he said.

She moved to him, lifted her hand, put it behind his head, pulled his face down toward her. His eyes closed and his mouth opened. His lips were soft and warm, but hesitant, and then something gave inside him and his slick tongue was curling along her teeth. He made a sound deep in his throat, a lost sound, a child's sound, and she felt it at the base of her stomach. A bristle of whiskers scraped at her cheek, fingers grasped at her back.

She held him for a moment, blood pulsing through her. Then, gently, she pushed him away and began to unbutton his top coat.

His eyes still closed, his arms at his sides, he raised his head toward the ceiling, like a sacrifice, waiting.

She eased the coat from his shoulders, and it fell to the floor.

CHAPTER NINETEEN

"Why?" Tom asked her.

"Why what?" said Lois.

"Why him."

"Not a huge supply of men in town, Tom."

"This one was married."

"He was nice. And he was hurting."

"Jesus Christ, Lois."

She shrugged. "You don't want to know, don't ask."

"Everyone in the world is hurting, one way or another. You gonna take care of 'em all?"

She lifted her chin. "I liked him," she said.

"Right." She had refilled his coffee. He took another sip. "How long did it last, the two of you?"

"The two of us? I saw him twice. The second time, his wife showed up, screaming and shouting. Next thing I know, he's gone, off to L.A."

"You never saw him again?"

"No."

"He was at the Plaza Hotel for a week before he left town. You see him then?"

"No."

"I can check at the hotel."

"You do that, Tom."

Tom nodded. "How long were the two of you at your place before Mrs. Whitfield showed up?"

"Maybe an hour."

"How'd she know about it?"

She shrugged. "Some nosy neighbor called her."

"How'd the neighbor know who to call?"

"People know him, here in town. He's famous."

"Which neighbor? Why?"

"Beats me."

"You tell anyone he was coming?"

"Why would I do that?"

"Yes or no."

"No."

Nodding, he stood up, away from the bar. "Okay. Thanks. What do I owe for the coffee?"

"On the house. Like our free lunch. You should come by sometime, Tom, and try out the free lunch."

"You know what they say about a free lunch, Lois."

"We got one here, so they're wrong."

"Sure they are."

He took a fifty cent piece from his pocket, put it on the bar. "Thanks again," he said.

CHAPTER TWENTY

A new day. The sun was shining, and Albuquerque and Lamy were behind him. Ahead of him, a half an hour away, lay Las Vegas and Dead Horse.

After three months in Los Angeles, it was strange to see the familiar New Mexico countryside go sliding by, the arroyos, the piñon-studded hills, the ragged mountains off in the distance, purple with shadow, green with ponderosa pine.

He remembered the first time he and Emily had seen it. After a weekend in Chicago at the Drake, they caught the westbound night train at Union Station. They had a private compartment and the first thing they did was make love, both of them laughing at their awkwardness within the tiny bed, foreheads and knees comically colliding. Afterward, they slept through most of the trip, through Illinois and Missouri and Kansas and the southeast corner of Colorado, and he awakened just as he felt the train begin to make a descent, the front of the compartment tilted slightly downward. Light was seeping into the room along the edges of the window shade.

He climbed down off the upper bed and lifted his robe from the hook by the door. In the lower bed, Emily was still asleep, curled toward the wall, her round white shoulder arcing above the sheet.

Swaying with the jostle of the train, he padded to the window and eased aside the shade.

What he saw made him tug on its bottom. The shade sprang up, snapping.

He turned, lifted Emily's robe from its hook, then padded back to her, sat down on the edge of the bed. He stroked her hair.

94

"Mmm," she said.

"Em," he said. "Emily?"

"Mmm?" Beneath the sheet, she stretched and turned. She opened her blue eyes, smiled up at him. "Mmm. What is it, darling?" She blinked. "Are we there?"

He bent down, kissed her forehead. "Come see this."

"See what?"

"Come on."

He stood up, giving her room. She yawned once, stretched again, then lightly flipped back the sheets and swung her legs off the bed. He handed her the robe and she slipped it on, over her black nightgown, as she stood. Taking her hand, he led her to the window.

For a moment she simply stared. "Oh my God," she said finally. "Where are we?"

"Raton Pass, I think. The conductor described it to me. He said we'd be here, right about now. If it is, we're just over the border from Colorado."

It was almost an aerial view. Below them, huge pine trees swept down a steep incline, down along ridges and knolls and rambling valleys. At the bottom the trees disappeared and the landscape opened up, spreading out in an enormous fan of yellow and red to the hazy blue mountains at the horizon.

"So we're in New Mexico?" she said. "That's New Mexico?"

"I think so."

"It's gorgeous. It's wonderful." She slipped her arm around his waist, looked up at him. "Oh, darling, we should forget Morocco, the south of Spain, all of it. We should buy ourselves a little ranch or a farm right here, and we should settle down and live happily ever after."

He smiled. "Farms are crops. Ranches are livestock."

"Oh, a ranch, then, absolutely. Lots of livestock. Bulls and burros and things."

He laughed. "Maybe we should wait until we see Las Vegas."

"We'll love it; I know we will." She leaned against him, lay her head on his chest, put her hand to her mouth, yawned again. "We *are* going to live happily ever after?"

He wrapped his arms around her. "It says so, right in the contract."

95

She turned to the window again and sighed. "It's so beautiful."
She looked up at him. "Do you know how it makes me feel?"

"How?"

"Well, to tell you the truth, darling, it makes me feel just a little
bit randy."

He smiled, slipped his hands down to the curve of her hips.
"What an amazing coincidence," he said.

• • •

There had been a contract, of course, and he had broken it.

Emily had believed she was marrying a writer. That had been
the bargain. She would provide the tea and crumpets; he would
provide the writing.

But he hadn't. For two years he had barely written a thing.

He'd made a few attempts, some character sketches, a couple
of limp vignettes. But, piece after piece, he'd tucked everything
into the drawer, telling himself that he'd work on it later. He
never had. It had been too easy not to.

At that first polo match, she had accused him of not writing in
order to punish her.

In a sense she had been right.

In the beginning he had wanted only to take a break. A small
break, away from the work. God knows, he had needed it. Ten
years of churning out crap for the pulps, day in, day out.

But the break kept stretching, down along the weeks and
months, and he had let it.

He had taken the freedom she gave him and, over time, out
of indolence and sloth, he had squandered it. And rather than
punish himself for wasting his talent, he had punished Emily for
providing the freedom. Punished her by destroying her dreams.

But of course, because they shared the dreams, in the end he
was punishing himself.

Maybe he had wanted that, too. Wanted to punish himself for
having made the deal in the first place.

It had been an attractive bargain. A beautiful woman. A
comfortable life stripped of cares and deadlines. All he had to
do, in return, was a little work.

But finally, ironically, stupidly, he had come to see freedom as liberation from the freedom that Emily offered. And he had rebelled.

He shook his head, looked out at the passing countryside.

He had made so many idiotic mistakes. The laziness, the drinking. Lois.

It had been insane to get involved with Lois. To spend that first night with her, to spend that catastrophic second night. Insane to spend those feverish moments, during that last hopeless week, in the back seat of the Lincoln, her breath damp in his ear, her skin slippery against his, the scent of her body filling the warm interior of the car, while every day he was pleading with Victor on the telephone, trying to persuade him to talk to Emily.

That first night had been another rebellion. Rebelling against Emily's constant fear of betrayal. And in the most stupid, most hateful way possible – by confirming it.

He shook his head.

He had to get back to work. He had to sit down every day and face the blank sheet, make the magic little marks. He had to lay off the booze. He had to stay away from Lois.

"Las Vegas! All out for Las Vegas!" The conductor, shuffling down the aisle.

The train was slowing.

Raoul stood and pulled his bag from the overhead rack.

Resting the bag on the seat, he looked out the window, at the town drifting alongside the train. It all seemed utterly familiar, as though nothing whatever had changed.

But of course everything had changed. Emily was gone.

His life at Dead Horse would never be the same.

PART TWO

CHAPTER TWENTY-ONE

Tom helped Maria into the passenger seat, shut the door, walked around the Dodge, and got into the driver's side. From her front porch, Mrs. Gomez waved at them.

He waved back, started the car. It was seven thirty. The sun had come up an hour ago, but the sky was overcast and milky.

"Daddy?" said Maria.

"Yeah?"

"Did you talk to Emily?"

"No, Sweetie. I talked to her father."

"And he's gonna tell her?"

"He said he would."

As he headed toward home, Maria stared out the windshield. "I think I should write her a letter," she said. She turned to him.

He nodded. "Be a nice thing to do."

"She didn't write back, you know. She just stopped. I wrote her two more letters and she never wrote back to me."

"Like you said, Sweetie. Probably she's real busy over there."

"I shouldn't say anything about Mr. Chervet, should I. In the letter."

"Say what about Mr. Chervet?"

"People at school, one of the kids, said he did it. He said Mr. Chervet got money from Mr. Whitfield, and he murdered Mrs. Whitfield so they could take all her fortune together."

"That's just stupid gossip, Sweetie. We don't know who did it."

"Emily liked Mr. Chervet. He taught her some words in Tagalong."

"In what?"

"Tagalong. That's what they talk in the Philipinos."

"The Philippines."

"The Philippines. Isn't that a funny name for a language, Daddy? Tagalong?"

He smiled at her. "Probably not to the folks in the Philippines."

"Tagalong," she said. She looked out the side window. "Tagalong." She turned to him. "They weren't bad words."

"The words he taught her?"

"Uh huh. They weren't bad words. They were words like 'house' and 'horse' and stuff."

"Glad to hear it," he said.

"What should I say? In the letter?"

"What you feel. You were sorry to hear about Mrs. Whitfield, right?"

"Of course."

"Then that's what you tell Emily."

She nodded, looked out the windshield. "Okay," she said. "That's what I'll tell her."

• • •

Back at the house, while Maria changed, Tom made some telephone calls. When she came back downstairs, he asked her if she wanted to play on the swing for a while, before he took her to school.

She looked off, in the direction of the swing set, and then turned back to him. "I don't think so. Is that okay?"

"That's fine," he said.

"I was looking at Emily's letters. Upstairs."

"Yeah?"

"Uh huh. I'm gonna write to her today for sure."

"Good."

• • •

99

When he got to the Department, Phil Sanchez was sitting at his desk, a pencil in his hand, a report form lying on the blotter. He looked up at Tom.

"Tom," he said.

"Phil." He took off the Stetson, hung it on the rack by the door. "You talk to the banks yesterday?"

"Yeah. She used the First National. She's got a safe deposit box there. I talked to Mr. Warburton and you were right – he can't open it without a court order."

Tom leaned back against the wall, crossed his arms.

"So like you said," Sanchez continued, "I went looking for Judge Baca. But he was out of town, and I didn't get to him until after five, and the bank was already closed. That was a good call, Tom. He hates Alonzo."

Tom nodded. "You get the order, Phil?"

"Right here." He opened his desk drawer, pulled out a folded sheet of paper, held it up.

Tom looked at his watch. Nine o'clock.

"Okay," he said. "You go give that to Warburton. Get the box opened. Make a list of everything inside."

"I don't take it with me? The stuff inside?"

"Case is officially closed."

"We looking for anything special?"

"A will. If it's there, copy it."

"The whole thing?"

"The whole thing." He looked over at Obregon's desk. "Where's Carlos?"

"Someone stole one of Manny Romero's pigs last night."

"Stole a pig?"

"That's what Manny says. Carlos went out to take a look. Listen, Tom, you're not still pissed off at me for yesterday? For letting Chervet go?"

He shook his head. "You didn't have much choice. I know that. Doesn't matter now anyway. I talked to Chervet last night."

"Yeah? You think he's straight?"

Tom shrugged. "He tells a good story."

• • •

100

A good story, he thought.

He was sitting back in his office chair. The door to the outer office was closed.

They all told good stories. Chervet, Lois, Carleton, Jane Templeton.

But the stories were like those houses you built out of cards, nothing holding them up except themselves. None of the stories were corroborated.

He believed Jane Templeton. Not necessarily the part about Mrs. Whitfield's first husband being such a bastard, but the rest sounded right. Mr. and Mrs. Whitfield in Paris, that was hearsay, but it sounded right.

Lois? Lois was Lois. Her story sounded right, too.

Carleton he wouldn't trust at high noon if the lawyer told him there was daylight outside.

Interesting thing, though. Carleton was there when the husband met Mrs. Whitfield. And he was there when the husband met Lois.

And Chervet?

He didn't know about Chervet. Man seemed to be real fond of Mrs. Whitfield. Stayed on after the husband left, ran the ranch for her.

But maybe he stayed on because he was working some kind of deal for the husband. And he had taken that Colt out of the woman's hand.

Well. There were a couple things he could check on….

He was reaching for the telephone when it rang. He picked it up.

"Sheriff Delgado."

"Sheriff, it's Wally Brown, at the station."

Tom had called him earlier, from the house. Now he asked him, "Mr. Whitfield show up?"

"Just got off the train."

"Anyone there to meet him?"

"Yep. That lawyer, Murray Carleton."

"Anyone with Carleton?"

"No sir. No one."

"Okay, Wally, thanks."

"Sheriff, is it true what they're saying?"

"Depends what they're saying."

"That Whitfield had that Filipino kill her. The wife."

"Wally, you worry about your trains and you let me worry about Mr. Whitfield."

"It's what they're saying, Sheriff."

"Be a good idea to stop listening. Thanks for the call."

Tom tapped the phone's button, dialed Zero, got the exchange, talked to Monica, asked her to call Dr. Hamilton.

After a moment, a woman's voice came on the line. "Hello?"

"Hello, Ma'am. This is Sheriff Tom Delgado. Like to speak to Dr. Hamilton?"

"This is Mrs. Hamilton. May I ask what it's about?"

"About one of his patients, Ma'am. Won't take long, I don't think."

"Hold on, please."

A few seconds passed. "Yes?"

"Dr. Hamilton?"

"Yes. Sheriff, is this about Emily Whitfield?"

"You heard she was dead?"

"Just a few minutes ago. A terrible thing. Terrible. You knew that she was my patient?"

"Yes, sir."

"Is it true that she committed suicide?"

"We don't know yet. Doctor, you prescribed some Luminal for Mrs. Whitfield last week, that right?"

"But I thought – she didn't overdose on the Luminal?"

"No, sir. Cause of death was a gunshot wound. Just checking into a few things. You did prescribe the Luminal?"

"Yes, I did. She complained of sleeplessness. I prescribed three weeks worth of tablets. I don't like prescribing it for any longer period."

"Why's that?"

"Do you know anything about Luminal, Sheriff?"

"Read a few things."

"It's a barbiturate. Phenobarbital. It can create a dependency. The withdrawal can be dangerous."

"So last week, that'd be the first time she came to you?"

"Yes. I opened my practice only a month ago."

102

"Doctor, one of the things I read was that this Luminal, it's not good for folks who're real depressed."

"I'm impressed, Sheriff. There are doctors who don't know that."

"So it's true?"

"Yes, it is. The drug can deepen the depression. But Mrs. Whitfield wasn't depressed. I specifically asked her about it."

"You knew she was going through a divorce?"

"Yes, she mentioned it, but she told me she was fine, except for the insomnia."

"What about mixing the stuff with alcohol?"

"It's a dangerous combination. The alcohol potentiates the Luminal, makes its effects stronger. Sheriff, are you saying that Mrs. Whitfield did mix them?"

"I got testimony says she did. Just about every day."

Dr. Hamilton said nothing for a moment. "She lied to me," he said finally.

"How's that?"

"I asked her about alcohol, naturally. She said she didn't drink. I believed her."

"I also got testimony says she's been taking pills since March."

"The same pills? Luminal?"

"Don't know."

Dr. Hamilton was silent.

"Doctor?" said Tom.

"Was she lying about the depression, too?"

"Yes, sir. I think she was."

"So you're suggesting that the Luminal deepened her depression, and that she committed suicide as a result?"

"No, sir. Not suggesting anything. What I'm trying to do here is find out as much as I can. I didn't know Mrs. Whitfield. I need to get some kind of a picture of who she was."

"She seemed a perfectly normal, rational person. If she hadn't, I'd never have prescribed the Luminal."

"But sounds like your prescription wasn't the first one she got."

"Yes, it does." He paused. "I liked her. She was a pleasant, attractive, sophisticated woman. A little nervous, perhaps, but I attributed that to the insomnia."

"I think she was going through a bad patch, and she didn't know how to handle it."

"Perhaps. May I suggest something to you, Sheriff?"

"Go ahead."

"There are three other doctors in town. Suppose I telephone them and ask about Mrs. Whitfield. If she was getting prescriptions from any of them, we can at least determine what she was taking."

"Good idea, Doctor. And if it was Luminal all this time?"

"She'd have developed a dependence and a tolerance. She'd need more of it to get the same effect."

"She'd be addicted."

"For all practical purposes, yes. I'll call them right now, Sheriff, and I'll get back to you as soon as I can."

"Appreciate it, Doctor."

Tom clicked the telephone and got Monica again, asked her to call Bradley Benson in Santa Fe. After a few moments, he got through to Benson's secretary. He told her who he was and she asked him to wait.

After another few moments, he heard, "This is Bradley Benson, Sheriff. How can I help you?"

CHAPTER
TWENTY-TWO

First off, Mr. Benson, I wanted to know if you heard about Mrs. Emily Whitfield."

"Her suicide? I was informed of it yesterday. A great pity. She was a fine woman."

"Who was it informed you?"

"Her husband's attorney. Murray Carleton."

"You talk to Mr. Carleton a lot?"

"From time to time. It's not uncommon in a divorce proceeding."

"Mrs. Whitfield's divorce. What were the grounds?"

"Mental cruelty. It's a matter of public record, Sheriff. We filed in February."

"She ever talk to you about any specific kind of mental cruelty?"

"I'm sorry, Sheriff, but any conversations I might've had with Mrs. Whitfield would be privileged. I wouldn't be at liberty to reveal them."

"She's dead, Mr. Benson."

"That changes nothing."

"You know if she wrote a new will?"

Benson said nothing.

Tom said, "Either she did or she didn't, Mr. Benson. I'm not asking for the details here."

"So far as I know," the lawyer said, "she didn't."

"She ever talk about it?"

"Once again, Sheriff, that would be in the category of privileged information."

"How'd she seem to you?"

"Seem?"

"She seem sad? Depressed?"

"She was going through a divorce. Most people find that a trying experience."

"She seem suicidal?"

"Sheriff, it's impossible for me to judge someone else's mental state."

"Uh huh. How'd you feel when you heard about the suicide?"

"My feelings would be irrelevant."

"Right," said Tom. "The divorce. It wasn't final yet?"

"No."

"When was it supposed to be?"

"In July."

"Okay, Mr. Benson. Thank you."

"You're welcome, Sheriff."

Tom hung up the phone.

Getting information out of a lawyer was like. . . .

Someone knocked at the door.

He called out, "Come in."

The door opened and Jane Templeton walked into the room.

A busy day.

He stood. "Hello, Ma'am."

Tom had been wrong about her clothes. She did have another dark outfit. Today she was wearing a gray blouse and a different gray skirt, longer than the first. Under her arm she carried a black leather purse. He saw that the skin beneath her eyes was still smudged.

"Hello, Sheriff. I'm not disturbing you?"

"Not a bit of it. Have a seat."

"Thank you."

She sat, putting the purse in her lap. "I just wanted to say goodbye."

He eased back into his chair. "You taking the afternoon train?"

"Yes."

"Mr. Whitfield's not gonna have a funeral?"

"He's sending…her home, to New York. To her mother."

Tom nodded.

106

"But before I left," she said, "I wanted to see if you'd learned anything. About Emily."

"No, Ma'am. Not a whole lot."

"Do you still believe that she was murdered?"

"Yes, Ma'am, I do."

"But who could've done it?"

"Don't know that yet."

"And why would anyone kill her?"

"I knew why, Ma'am, I'd know who."

Her eyelids fluttered and she looked down. "Yes, of course. It was a stupid question."

"Not so stupid." When she looked up, he smiled. "Been asking it myself."

"Do you think you'll ever know, Sheriff?"

"Can't say, Ma'am. I hope so. Like I said, I don't want that little girl of hers to go on thinking her mother died that way. But the case is closed, officially. I can poke around, ask some questions, make a nuisance of myself. But I can't do a whole lot more unless I come up with something solid."

She nodded, opened her purse, pulled out a slip of paper. "This is my telephone number in New York. If you do learn anything, would you call me? You can reverse the charges, of course."

He smiled again. "I figure we can afford a call to New York. Soon as I have anything, I'll let you know."

"Thank you, Sheriff." She put the paper on the desk. "And would you mind terribly if I called here from time to time?"

"I won't be needing any reminders, Ma'am."

"I know that. It's more for my sake than for yours – so I can feel as though I'm actually doing something. Would that be all right?"

"Course it would. Anytime."

"Thank you." She stood, and so did Tom, and he came around the desk. She held out her hand and he shook it.

He said, "You take care of yourself, Ma'am."

"And you, Sheriff."

He walked her to the door, opened it, held it for her. He saw Phil Sanchez waiting out there, a folded sheet of paper in his hand. He watched Miss Templeton cross the outer office, and

107

then he turned to Sanchez and waved him in. Just as Sanchez stepped inside, the telephone rang.

Tom shut the door, crossed over to his desk, sat down on it, picked up the phone. "Sheriff Delgado."

"Sheriff, this is Don Hamilton. Dr. Hamilton. I spoke with the others. One of them had been prescribing Luminal to Mrs. Whitfield until last week. He cut her off then – no tapering, no concern whatever for the effects of withdrawal. It's criminal."

"Criminal, but not illegal."

"No. Not illegal. I feel very badly about this – it should never have happened. But she certainly didn't look like an addict. And she was completely persuasive."

"Yes, sir. I understand."

Tom heard the man sigh. "Sheriff, if she was depressed, and she was addicted to Luminal, than it's entirely possible that she did commit suicide."

"Why use a gun when you got a whole bottle full of pills?"

"I couldn't answer that. But barbiturate poisoning doesn't make for an attractive death. Vomiting, convulsions."

"Gun shot doesn't make for an attractive death either."

"Well. No. Of course not."

"I do appreciate your making those calls."

"Is it at all helpful, Sheriff, knowing about the Luminal?"

"Helps me make up that picture I was talking about. Thank you, Doctor."

"Yes. You're welcome. Goodbye."

Tom hung up, turned to Sanchez. Sanchez said, "What did –"

"That the list?" said Tom, nodding to the paper in his hand.

"Yes, sir." He handed it over.

Tom opened it. Three necklaces, four brooches, three rings. One deed to Dead Horse Ranch, in Mrs. Whitfield's name. One deed to a townhouse in New York City, also in her name. One last will and testament.

"You copied the will?" he asked Sanchez

"Right here." He reached into his shirt pocket, pulled out another folded sheet, handed it to Tom.

Tom unfolded it. Only two simple lines. "That's it?"

"That's it."

"The original's in her handwriting?"

"Same writing as her signature."

Tom read it.

Being of sound mind and body, I, Emily Whitfield, do hereby leave all of my worldly goods, all monies, possessions, and property, and any interest accruing therefrom, to my husband, Raoul Whitfield.

It was dated July, 1933, and it was signed by Mrs. Whitfield. Two witnesses had also signed it. One was Jane Templeton. The other was Murray Carleton.

CHAPTER
TWENTY-THREE

Sitting on the bottom row of the empty bleachers, Raoul looked out across the polo field. Amid the tall grasses, Johnny Archuleta perched in its tiny seat, the ranch's yellow tractor towed the reel of bulky, whirring mowing blades. Smoke puffed from the stack. The field hadn't been tended since last October, and growing in the grass were spindly stalks of penstemon, their blossoms lavender and pink and bright red, like flecks of blood.

Beyond the tractor, bouncing up the rutted dirt road, came an old Dodge police car.

Sheriff Delgado.

Raoul sat there and remembered that first polo match, when the grass had been emerald green and closely cropped. He remembered Diamond beneath him, muscles bunching, hooves thudding, as they raced toward the ball. Remembered the mallet whacking against it, the ball shooting across the goal line. The incredible surge of triumph he'd felt, Emily waving to him, ecstatic....

The Dodge parked fifty yards away and Sheriff Delgado stepped out, shut the door, adjusted his Stetson, hitched up his gun belt comfortably, and then started toward Raoul.

He moved slowly and deliberately, a big man, barrel-chested, a bit overweight, his legs slightly bowed.

Raoul stood.

Coming around the trunk of the big piñon, Delgado touched the brim of his hat. "Mr. Whitfield."

Raoul held out his hand. "Sheriff Delgado, isn't it?"

They shook.

"We met last year," Delgado said. "The Fourth of July."

"I remember now."

"Kind of expected to find Mr. Carleton out here. Didn't pass him on the road." He looked around the field, glanced at the utility shack behind the bleachers as though Murray might be crouching inside it.

"You knew that Murray met me at the station?" Raoul asked him.

Delgado smiled. "Folks talk, Mr. Whitfield."

Raoul smiled back. "So it seems. Murray's gone, Sheriff. He had to drive down to Santa Fe. Please, take a seat."

The two of them sat on the bench.

"Only fair to tell you, Mr. Whitfield, that you don't have to talk to me without him here."

Raoul smiled. "Will I need him, Sheriff?"

"Doubt it. Just trying clear up a few things."

"Murray told me the case was closed."

"Just filling in a few holes."

Raoul nodded. "What can I do for you?"

"Well, first off, I wanted to say I'm real sorry about your wife. What I hear, she was a fine woman."

"She was. Thank you."

"Okay. Now you just correct me, Mr. Whitfield, if I get anything wrong."

Raoul nodded.

"It was February you left for California, that right?"

"Yes. The middle of February."

"And it was a little while before that, about a week, that Mrs. Whitfield showed up at Lois Bell's house."

Raoul took a deep breath, blew it out through pursed lips, lowered his head. "One of the biggest mistakes I've ever made." He turned to Delgado. "If I could take back one single moment of my life, Sheriff, it would be that one."

Delgado nodded. "She's a good looking girl, Lois."

"I don't blame Lois. I blame myself. Emily and I had been having difficulties. In the marriage. But we'd had difficulties before, and we'd always worked them out. I was drunk that night, and I was foolish. I was self-destructive. If it hadn't been Lois, it would've been someone else, I expect."

111

Delgado nodded. "Just who do you think it was, Mr. Whitfield, told your wife about Lois?"

"I've no idea. I'd always assumed it was one of Lois's neighbors."

"Why would a neighbor do that?"

"As you say, people talk. A small town, small town jealousies, small town hatreds. But as to why in this case, I just don't know."

"You ever see Lois again, after that night?"

Raoul looked at him. "Yes. A few times. Before I left. I was still reeling, Sheriff. Emily was down in Santa Fe and she wouldn't talk to me. My whole life was falling apart. In a sense, Lois was the only thing I had left."

"She told me she never saw you."

"I expect she was trying to protect me."

"From what?"

Raoul smiled. "Probably from you. Your judgment of me. In her own way, Sheriff, Lois is a fine girl. It's not her fault that I was such a wreck in February."

"Why'd you go out to California?"

"I wanted to get away. Get away from everything. And I thought that maybe, if I gave Emily some time, some distance, she might reconsider. That maybe she and I would be able to work things out."

"You talk to her from there?"

"I tried, but she refused to take the calls." He shook his head. "I wish now that I hadn't gone. If I'd stayed, Emily might never have done what she did."

Delgado nodded. "You think she killed herself."

Raoul frowned. "Of course she killed herself."

"Funny, though. Mr. Carleton told me she was unhappy about not having her daughter around. But I hear the daughter was supposed to be here in a few weeks."

"Emily probably wasn't thinking too clearly."

"Mr. Carleton explained that. But then there's the situation with the pistol."

"The pistol?"

"Well now," said Delgado. He pulled his big revolver from

its holster. "The wound was in her left side. According to Mr. Chervet, she was holding her Colt—"

He stopped and said, "This okay with you, Mr. Whitfield? We can forget about it, it's gonna be too hard on you."

"I'm fine, Sheriff. Thank you. Go ahead."

"She was holding it like this." Delgado reversed the pistol, holding down the hammer with the fingers of his left hand, and he grasped the grip with his right hand, his thumb in the trigger guard. "Now, she does that, and it's just possible she can shoot herself in the left side, down here. See?" He demonstrated.

Raoul nodded.

"But," said Delgado, "it's not a natural kind of thing to do."

He put the pistol back in the holster. "Why shoot yourself down there? People shoot themselves, they try to do it in the heart. Or maybe they put the barrel in their mouth. And the thing is, most women, they commit suicide, they don't use a gun. They use pills, if they got any. And Mrs. Whitfield, she had enough Luminal to kill four or five people. That's a sleeping pill."

"I know." He frowned. "I didn't know she was taking it."

"It's right there on the night stand, in the bedroom."

"I haven't been into the bedroom yet, Sheriff. As you might understand, it's not something I'm looking forward to. How long had she been taking it?"

"Since about the time you left."

Raoul looked off across the polo field. And there was Emily waving to him from a mirrored, phantom set of bleachers across the field. Wildly happy, jumping up and down, her hand semaphoring back and forth

"You know about the gun?" Delgado asked him. "The Colt?"

Raoul turned to him. "I bought it for her. It was a joke, more than anything else. Something else I truly wish I'd never done."

"You got any idea why she might use the Colt and not the pills?"

"I can't explain it," said Raoul. "But obviously, for whatever reason, she chose to use the pistol. And if she were holding it that way—"

"Well, yeah," said Delgado. "But see, we only got Mr. Chervet's word for the way she was holding the gun. He took it out of her hand. No one else saw it."

113

"What about fingerprints?"

"Prints on the trigger were smudged."

"Sheriff, I've known Victor Chervet for most of my life. If he says something, it's the truth. He's an honest man."

"You grew up with him, that right?"

"In the Philippines."

"Got him a job in New York. Got him a job out here. I guess he'd be pretty grateful."

"What are you saying?"

"Making a comment is all."

"A provocative comment."

"Not trying to provoke anyone."

Raoul's laugh was harsh. "Christ, Sheriff, do you think I'm an idiot? I'm a writer. I've been inventing people like you for over twenty years. Cops, cons, private detectives. Shrewd county sheriffs. There's nothing you can say – nothing – that I haven't already put into someone's mouth."

"Must save you a lot of time. Making conversation."

"Wherever you're going with this, I've already been there. A hundred times. A thousand times. But just so you'll know, Victor Chervet was probably more fond of Emily than he was of me. He'd never hurt her."

"Not even if someone paid him –"

"Not in any circumstances. And here's something else. We were separated, Emily and I. We had our problems."

"Like Lois Bell."

"Like Lois Bell. But I loved my wife. Your wife, Sheriff – what was her name? Carla?"

"Doesn't matter what my wife's name was."

"The fact is, she committed –"

"Fact is, my wife doesn't enter into this."

"The fact is, you lost your wife. You must have some idea how I feel. Emily's death hit me like a fist in the chest. I wouldn't, I couldn't kill her. Not on my own, not with someone's help. Have you got that?"

"I got it."

"Good. Then I suppose we can end this."

"Guess we can."

"Goodbye, Sheriff."

His face expressionless, Delgado stood, touched the brim of his hat, and turned. He walked off toward the Dodge.

Raoul watched him get in, start the car, reverse it, swing it back along the road, and then go bouncing and bucking toward the entrance to the ranch.

When the car was out of sight, he turned toward the utility shed and called out, "He's gone."

Lois opened the door, stepped out, closed it, walked around the bleachers to Raoul. She laid her hand on his shoulder.

"You want me to go, Sugar?" she said. "You want to take me back to town?"

He put his hands on her hips, lowered his head, gently pressed the side of his face against her stomach.

Slowly, she stroked his hair. "Is there something I can do?"

He sat back, looked up at her. "Yes," he said.

CHAPTER
TWENTY-FOUR

On Saturday morning, after breakfast, Maria asked Tom to read the letter she'd written.

Dear Emily,
I heard about what happened to your mother Mrs. Whitfield and I wanted to tell you I was very sorry to hear about it. Your mother was a very nice person and I liked her a lot even tho I only met her one time. I am very sorry for your unhappiness. I hope everything is okay for you in France. And I hope I will see you some time in the future.
Your friend,
Maria Delgado

"Sounds real good," he said, and handed the letter back. "Emily'll be happy to get it."

"Is everything spelled okay?"

"Don't think *tho* is right. T-h-o. Pretty sure it's t-h-o-u-g-h."

Maria put the letter on the table, lifted her pen, and carefully wrote in the letters. For a moment, still holding the pen, she studied what she'd done, and then looked at Tom. "I better do it over again."

"Might be a good idea."

She started to walk away, but then turned back to him.

"They're still saying it at school, Daddy," she said. "Everyone."

"Saying what?"

"That Mr. Chervet did it."

"Sweetie, we just don't know who did it. Officially, Mrs. Whitfield did it herself."

"They say Mr. Whitfield paid money to people to say she did it herself."

"You think I got paid money?"

"Of course not."

He nodded. "Like I say, we don't know."

She frowned at him. "How come people gossip so much, Daddy?"

"Don't know for sure, Sweetie. Everybody's got a little bit of evil inside him, I guess. Gossip is a way for all of 'em to share it, and pretend it's something else."

"Gossip is evil?"

"Kind of, yeah. Takes pleasure in someone else being unhappy, doesn't it? Or hopes he's gonna be unhappy."

"Everyone's got evil inside him? Even you?"

"Not me. I'm perfect. You ever hear me gossip?"

"Unh unh."

"There you are."

She laughed.

"You go fix up your letter, Sweetie, and I'll mail it after I drop you off."

"Do I have to go to Mrs. Gomez's today?"

"I got business, Sweetie. But I'll pick you up in the afternoon, if I can."

"When?"

"Around one. If I can, I'll take you to lunch."

"Really?"

"If I can, I will."

• • •

Back in his office, Tom told Phil Sanchez about yesterday's conversation with Raoul Whitfield.

"You think he paid Chervet to do it?" Phil asked him.

"Don't know," said Tom, leaning back in his chair. "He tells a good story, like the rest of 'em. One thing, though. He wasn't surprised when I asked about his wife showing up at Lois Bell's house. Wasn't surprised I knew about it."

117

"Carleton told him?"

"Coulda been Carleton. Coulda been Chervet, coulda been Lois."

"He's only been back for a day, Tom. You think he's already started up with Lois again?"

"Good question." He sat up, leaned forward, picked up the telephone, dialed Zero, and then waited as the line rang at the exchange.

Sanchez held out his hands, palms showing, What?

Tom held up a finger.

When someone finally answered, it was Stella. "How can I help you?"

Tom would have preferred Monica, but you went with what you had.

"Stella, this is Sheriff Tom Delgado. I got—"

"Hello, Sheriff."

"Yeah, hello, Stella. Listen, I got a question for you."

"What question?"

"Lois Bell, on Rincon Street. She own a telephone?"

It had been only a year ago since Tom was inside the house, but except for what he and Lois had done, he couldn't remember any of the details.

"I don't know, Sheriff. That's something I'd have to check up on."

"Could you do that for me?"

"Okay," she said. "You wanna hold on?"

"Sure."

He glanced at Sanchez, who was smiling. Like every officer in the department, Sanchez had dealt with Stella.

"Sheriff?"

"Right here, Stella."

"Uh huh. She does. Lois Bell, 112 Rincon." She gave him the phone number. He wrote it down.

"Okay, Stella," he said. "Now. You keep a record of all the long distance calls come into town, right?"

"Uh huh. We keep like a log."

"Could you check and see if any calls went to Lois Bell's number? This'd be from February till now. And check and see if she made any long distance calls herself."

118

"Check on the ones coming in and the ones going out?"

"That's right."

"You want them both from February till now?"

"Right."

"That's a long time, Sheriff."

"Three months, Stella."

"But it's two separate books. I'm gonna have to look through both of them, and it's gonna take me a while."

"That's okay. You just get back to me when you find out. Oh, and Stella?"

"Yeah?"

"Check on any long distance calls going into the Cantina, too. And out of it."

"Uh huh. The Cantina. I'm writing it down. You want that from February too?"

"Yeah."

"It's gonna take me a while, Sheriff."

"I know that, Stella. I appreciate the help."

"Okay. Just so you know. I'll call you back when I find out."

"Thank you." He hung up the phone, held up his finger again to Sanchez, then tapped the button. When he got the tone, he dialed the number that Stella had given him for Lois. No one answered.

He hung up and sat back. "When I talked to Whitfield," he told Sanchez, "he admitted he saw Lois after his wife came to her house. In that week before he left."

"Lois never saw him, I thought."

"What she told me."

"So why'd she lie about it?"

"Trying to protect him, he says."

"From what?"

"What I thought about him."

Sanchez frowned. "You figure Lois really cares what anyone thinks about anything?"

He smiled. "Not so's you'd notice."

"And even if Whitfield did call her, what's that tell us?"

"Tells us Whitfield was keeping in touch."

Sanchez frowned. "You don't think Lois did it, Tom? Killed Mrs. Whitfield?"

119

"Carleton says they were together that night. They both got alibis."

"Maybe they both did it? Together?"

Tom considered that. He wouldn't put anything past Murray Carleton. But Lois? Lois was hard, but probably not hard that way. "It'd surprise me some," he admitted. "But I been surprised before."

• • •

Tom took care of some other business, but when an hour passed and Stella still hadn't called, he drove over to the Cantina and found Roy Enfield, the owner, setting up for lunch. Enfield told him that Lois had called in sick yesterday.

"She do that a lot?" Tom asked him.

"Never," said Enfield. He was in his sixties, tall and thin and stooped. His small brown eyes were crafty; his cheeks were withered and stubbled with white. "Surprised the hell outta me, Tom. Never been sick a day in her life. I had to get Patsy to fill in for her. And wasn't Patsy tickled about that."

"When did Lois call in?"

"After the lunch shift. Around two."

"She working tonight?"

"Nope. Asked me for the two days off. Says she got a bad flu."

"She sound sick?"

"She coughed some. She could be. Who knows? But she never did call in sick before."

"Okay, Roy. Thanks."

"Lois in trouble, Sheriff?"

"Just checkin' on some things."

"Confidential, is it?"

"How do you mean?"

"I shouldn't tell Lois you been asking for her?"

Tom smiled. "You tell her whatever you want."

• • •

On his way back to the department, he stopped at Lois's house on Rincon Street and knocked on the door. No one answered.

120

The house was silent and still, abandoned.

When he got back to the office, Phil Sanchez told him that Stella had called with the information. Sanchez had written it all down.

There had been no long distance calls coming into, or going out from, the Cantina. On her own telephone, Lois had made three calls, two in March, one in April, all to the same number in Los Angeles.

Since the last week in February there had been at least one long distance call made to her phone every week. The last call had been made on Thursday morning, at nine o'clock. All of them had come from that same Los Angeles number. It was the number Tom had called from Dead Horse, at eight thirty on Thursday morning, to let Raoul Whitfield know about his wife.

CHAPTER
TWENTY-FIVE

The next day, Sunday, Tom made pancakes and fried eggs, Maria's favorite breakfast.

It was raining, a slow steady drizzle outside the windows, the sky so grim and gray that he left the kitchen lights on while they ate.

"The Acostas got a brand new puppy," Maria told him, using her fork to waltz a chunk of pancake through a pool of syrup.

"That right?"

"A collie. You should see it, Daddy. It's really cute." She tucked the chunk of pancake into her mouth.

"Collie's a nice dog," he said.

She swallowed. "Don't you think we should get a dog?"

"Told you, Sweetie. When you're older."

"Jerry Acosta's only eight."

"His mother's home all day. Puppy like that needs to have someone around."

"So we can't get a dog until when? When I finish high school?"

He smiled. "Maybe a little sooner."

"When?"

"When I can leave the two of you alone together."

"I'm already ten years old."

"Ten already?"

"So when am I gonna be old enough?"

"We'll see."

"Daddy —"

In the living room, the telephone rang.

"Be right back," Tom told her.

He wiped his mouth, set the paper towel on the table, got up, walked from the kitchen into the living room, picked up the phone. "Sheriff Delgado."

"Sheriff, this is Wally Brown."

"Morning, Wally. What can I do for you?"

"I just thought you'd want to know."

"Know what?"

"That Filipino. Chervet. Mr. Whitfield dropped him off here and he's waiting for the eastbound train."

"How do you know the eastbound train?"

"I sold him the ticket myself. To New York, through Chicago. And Sheriff?"

"Yeah?"

"The funeral home. Morrison's. They delivered a coffin. Mrs. Whitfield's coffin. It's going to New York on the same train."

Tom looked at his watch. Eight fifteen. The train arrived in an hour.

"Okay, Wally. Thank you."

"Anything you want me to do?"

"Like what, Wally? Make one of those citizen's arrests?"

"I don't know, Sheriff. I was only asking."

"No, Wally, thanks, but I don't want you to do anything. I appreciate the phone call."

"Just trying to do my duty."

"I know that. Thank you."

Tom tapped the button, called Mrs. Gomez, asked her if she could watch over Maria for an hour or so. She said she'd be happy to. He called Phil Sanchez at home, asked him to pick up Maria and drive her to Mrs. Gomez's place before he came to the office. Phil said he'd be right over.

Tom went back into the kitchen. "Sorry, Sweetie. I gotta go soon. Business. Phil Sanchez is coming over, and he'll take you to Mrs. Gomez's."

"We're not gonna go to Mass?"

"Maybe. This won't take long, probably."

"Is it about Mr. Whitfield?"

"Yeah. It could be important."

"If I had a dog, you know, it could protect me while you were gone."

"And who'd protect the dog?"

"That's not funny, Daddy."

He smiled at her. "When you get older, Sweetie."

• • •

By the time Tom reached the station, fifteen minutes later, the rain was rattling down. A stream of run-off gushed from the broken gutter along the building's northeast corner, wobbled through the air, mushroomed against the pavement.

He parked the Dodge in the lot, adjusted his hat, buttoned up the oiled canvas slicker, opened the door, and stepped out into the downpour. A chill wind was blowing. He slammed the door shut and went splashing through the puddles to the front door.

Inside the station, he took off the Stetson, snapped its brim against his palm to shake loose the water, shoved it back on.

The air here was warm. An older couple sat huddled at one of the benches near the woodstove.

No Chervet.

He glanced at the ticket booth and saw that Wally Brown was inside there, waving at him. Wally pointed theatrically toward the platform outside.

Tom crossed the room, opened the door, stepped out onto the covered platform. He looked around.

Chervet sat alone, a small figure at the end of a bench to Tom's right. Just beyond the bench, raised on a big metal dolly, was a coffin, its black wood gleaming, its brass handles shining.

Rain drummed against the roof, but the sound of Tom's boots against the thick wooden slats of the flooring made Chervet turn toward him. He stood, taking off his hat and holding it in both hands.

Tom nodded. "Mr. Chervet."

"Good morning, Sheriff."

"Mind if I join you for a minute?"

"No, sir. Please sit down."

Tom lowered himself to the center of the bench, his slicker creaking, and Chervet sat back down, still holding his hat in his hands.

"Taking a trip?" Tom asked him.

124

"Yes, sir." He nodded to the coffin. "I am taking her home. To her family." He frowned. "That is permitted, no?"

"Course it is. You plan on coming back?"

For a moment Chervet looked off through the gray curtains of rain, across the dull silver tracks where the rain spattered into spray. Beyond them, to the east, the hills were invisible in the clouds.

Then he turned to Tom. "Sheriff," he said, "on Mindanao there is a village. Close to my family's farm, you understand?"

"Sure."

"In this village, many years ago, there are two cousins. Manuel and Luis. And one day they are playing cards with two other men, and there is an argument. One of the other men, a big man, he is very angry at Manuel, and he wants to fight with him. He wants to hurt him. And Luis, he wants to stop this. So he says, 'Do not fight with Manuel! He has a knife!'"

Tom nodded.

"Manuel," said Chervet, "he has no knife, but the angry man, he does not know this, and so he and his friend go away."

Chervet looked off again, toward the east, and then turned back to Tom. "Everyone in the village, they think this is a very fine story, a very funny story. They know that Manuel, he never has a knife. So after this, when he comes into the village, they all say to him, 'Manuel, where is your knife?' And Manuel, he always says, 'But I have no knife!'"

The wind slapped a cold gust of rain onto the platform, spraying Tom's cheek.

Chervet didn't notice the rain. "For a long time this happens," he said. "For years. And Manuel, he gets more and more angry. 'I have no knife! I have no knife!' he says to them. He does not come into town so much now. And then one day, after months, he comes in again. It is raining, a day like today. And everyone asks about this knife, of course. And now he screams at them. 'I have no knife!' And there, in the center of the village, he takes off his clothes, very fast. He takes them off, all of them, to show he has no knife. And he stands there in the rain naked, and he screams at them, 'I have no knife!' And now no one laughs. And then he runs away without his clothes, into the jungle. He never comes back. They find him, his body; they find it later. He starves to death."

"You're not coming back," said Tom.

"No, sir. No. Yesterday I go to the McAllister Store, on Main Street. Mr. Whitfield, he sends me to buy some things for the ranch. Mr. McAllister, he tells me to leave his store. He will not sell me these things."

"I could talk to Jim McAllister."

"It is not Mr. McAllister only, sir. It is the town. They all think I hurt Mrs. Whitfield."

If Chervet left, he might be taking with him all the answers Tom needed. He had been in the Dead Horse ranch house that night. He had been the last person to see Mrs. Whitfield alive, and the first to see her in the morning, dead.

It was possible, too, that the town was right, and he had killed the woman.

But Tom didn't think so. It seemed to him that Chervet's quiet grief was genuine.

"What're you gonna do, Mr. Chervet?" Tom asked. "When you get to New York?"

"I have some money, sir. I save it over years. I think maybe I go back to the island."

"To Mindanao."

"Yes, sir."

"Be faster, wouldn't it, take a boat from California?"

"Someone must go with her, sir." He looked toward the coffin. "Someone must be with her on her journey home."

"How come Mr. Whitfield doesn't go?"

"He is very busy now, sir. There are many things to do on the ranch."

Sighing, Tom took off his hat, ran his hand back through his hair. "Well now, Mr. Chervet," he said, and put the hat back on. "I'm sorry people been giving you a hard time. People are ignorant sometimes."

Chervet blinked and then looked off, through the rain, across the tracks. The rain drummed against the roof.

"One thing, though," said Tom.

The man turned to him. He blinked again. "Yes, sir?"

"Thinking back to the night Mrs. Whitfield died. You sure you

126

didn't hear that pistol go off? A big weapon, Mr. Chervet. A Colt .45. Makes one hell of a noise."

Chervet's face was without expression. "I did not hear it, sir. I swear it. I am a very heavy sleeper. And the walls, they are very thick."

"And you don't know who telephoned Mrs. Whitfield, told her about her husband being at Lois Bell's?"

"No, sir."

"Did Mrs. Whitfield ever talk to Lois Bell?"

"At the house, sir. The house of Lois Bell. I tell you this."

"Any other time? Miss Bell ever telephone Mrs. Whitfield?"

"No, sir. Mostly I am answering the telephone. She never calls Mrs. Whitfield."

"Mrs. Whitfield never telephoned Miss Bell?"

"No, sir. I think I would know of this."

"You think Mrs. Whitfield committed suicide, Mr. Chervet?"

His face still empty, Chervet nodded. "Yes, sir. I think this is what happens. I think she is very unhappy."

"Okay. Thank you, Mr. Chervet." Tom stood up and held out his hand.

Chervet rose from the bench, still holding onto the brim of his hat, and took it.

"You speak any Spanish, Mr. Chervet?"

"A little, sir. From here and from the island."

"Well. Vaya con Dios."

Chervet bobbed his head. "Thank you. And to you, sir. Go with God."

CHAPTER
TWENTY-SIX

Time passed.
There weren't many more people to talk to, weren't many more leads to follow.

Now and then, when Tom had a few hours free, he drove out the road to Dead Horse and stopped at the other ranches scattered along it, hidden among the hills. On the night that Mrs. Whitfield died, no one had seen or heard anything strange. The ranch houses were all some distance from each other, and at one o'clock in the morning, when it happened, everyone was asleep.

Lois Bell quit her job at the Cantina and moved out to Dead Horse. Twice, Tom saw the two of them in town, her and Whitfield, hanging onto each other and laughing. It wasn't illegal, of course, wasn't necessarily even immoral. But for Tom it just wasn't right – not after what Whitfield had said about loving his wife.

Tom knew that they'd seen him, but they ignored him, or pretended to.

There was other business to attend to. Old man Eakins died, a heart attack at his tiny farm, and no one found him for a week. Some cattle were rustled up north, in what turned out to be one Santiago cousin stealing from another. In July, on Route 66, an Ilfield Department Store delivery truck smashed into an old Ford carrying a family of Okies. All of the people in the Ford were killed – mother, father, three young children. Their possessions had been roped to the roof of the car, and when Tom got there, they were lying all over the road – battered cardboard boxes, bulging at their ruptured seams with cheap, worn clothing that still smelled of laundry soap.

Miss Templeton called a few times, from New York, but Tom had nothing to tell her.

Even if she hadn't called, he would have kept thinking about Emily Whitfield. Twice he drove all the way out to Dead Horse and then down along the dirt road that led to the ranch house. He stopped the car when he could see out across the polo field to the house beyond it. Probably the two of them knew he was there; probably they were watching his car, just as he watched the house. He didn't care.

He sat there and he thought about the woman, thought about her the way Miss Templeton and Victor Chervet had described her. A little headstrong, maybe, but elegant and bright and passionate. Brave, too, and loyal. Flying over France with Whitfield in the middle of the night. Coming out here to New Mexico with him, miles from New York, miles from Paris, fixing up that studio, buying him that library.

Maybe, like Chervet said, she was a jealous woman. But Tom figured her husband was the kind of man who probably didn't have much trouble making women feel jealous.

He remembered her as she had been on the Fourth of July, when the wind had fluttered her yellow silk dress. Beautiful and slim, completely focused on her daughter, beaming as she handed over that great pink swirl of cotton candy....

• • •

On August 27, the details of Emily Whitfield's will were made public. As Tom had expected, her entire estate went to her husband, including the townhouse in New York and the jewelry in the safe deposit box.

Two weeks later, like most of the people in town, Tom learned about the wedding from the daily paper.

• • •

When Tom arrived at Dead Horse, he saw that a corner of the polo field was cluttered with cars. Murray Carleton's Packard was one of them, parked closest to the house. But the other cars weren't the expensive vehicles Tom would have expected – the

129

Cadillacs and Lincolns and Auburn sedans of the town's rich folks. They were old Fords and Chevys, decrepit pick-up trucks, even a few delivery vans. Two of the county's school buses, their blue paint fading now, sat side by side, bodies angled, long hoods nuzzling each other, like snouts.

All the guests were gathered around a big white canopy on the far side of the bleachers. Tom parked the Dodge and walked across the grass.

People were drinking from paper cups or shoveling chunks of wedding cake from paper plates into their mouths. He nodded to the ones he knew, mostly customers of the Cantina, and they stopped eating and drinking and they turned to each other – wondering, probably, why he was here.

At the entrance to the canopy, he looked through the crowd and saw Whitfield and Lois standing by the bar, drinks in their hands. Whitfield wore a tuxedo dinner jacket; Lois wore a white dress. Wearing a tuxedo of his own, Murray Carleton stood beside them and grinned. Just as Tom stepped into the canopy's shade, Carleton saw him, tapped Whitfield on the shoulder, and then started walking toward Tom, shouldering past the guests. Whitfield and Lois watched. Whitfield took a sip of his drink.

As Carleton reached him, Tom touched the brim of his hat. "Mr. Carleton."

"This is a private party, Sheriff, on private property."

"Wedding party, I heard."

"That's correct."

"Kind of sudden, isn't it? Only two weeks now since Mrs. Whitfield's will got read."

"What's your point?"

"Doesn't look real good, does it? Makes people think."

"Think what? That Raoul had something to do with Emily's death?"

"Something like that."

"If he had, wouldn't getting married be the last thing he'd do?"

Tom smiled. "Too clever for me. I'm just a county sheriff. Funny thing, though."

"What's that?"

"Couple months ago, I asked you if Mrs. Whitfield had a will.

130

The other Mrs. Whitfield. Emily Whitfield. I recollect correctly, you told me you believed so."

"You recollect correctly."

"The thing is, though, you signed that will as a witness. Probably dictated, too. It reads like something a lawyer would say."

"Sheriff, do you have any idea how many wills I've dealt with, one way or the other?"

"How many?"

"Hundreds. I can't remember every single one of them."

Tom nodded. "Something else I was wondering about."

"What?"

"You being here. Thought you and Lois had a thing going. Gave each other alibis for the night Mrs. Whitfield got killed. The other Mrs. Whitfield."

"She didn't get killed. She committed suicide. And not that it's any of your business, but Lois has been a friend of mine for some time. So has Raoul, as you know. I'm very happy for the two of them."

"Didn't you say Emily Whitfield was a friend of yours?"

"She was. But life goes on, Sheriff."

"Not for everyone."

Carleton frowned. "Do you have a warrant of some sort?"

"Nope."

"Then unless you have some legitimate reason to be here—"

"Just curious, is all. Mr. Whitfield there, he told me he was all broke up about his wife's death. Looks like he made a nice recovery."

"The case is closed. Your presence here constitutes harassment of my client. As his lawyer, I'm obliged to discuss this with the District Attorney."

"Uh huh. Well, good to see you, Mr. Carleton. You give my regards to Mr. and Mrs. Whitfield."

CHAPTER
TWENTY-SEVEN

On Monday morning, Tom was sitting again in his office, talking to Phil Sanchez.

"How many people were out there?" Sanchez asked him.

"Maybe a hundred. County school buses drove a bunch of 'em out."

"Who paid for that?"

"Whitfield. I checked."

"Whole thing probably cost him a pretty penny."

"He's got a lot of those right now."

"So what do we do, Tom?"

"Don't see there's much we *can* do. Maybe it's time to pack it in." He shook his head. "But I keep thinking about that little girl. The daughter. She's gonna think, for the rest of her life, that her mother thought dying was better than seeing her again."

Sanchez hesitated. "No disrespect, Tom—"

Someone knocked brusquely at the office door.

Tom called out, "Come in."

The door swung open and Peter Alonzo, the assistant District Attorney, strode into the room. Sanchez stood.

Alonzo's plump mouth was thin now. He glared at Tom. "We need to talk, Sheriff."

"Peter," said Tom. "You know Deputy Sanchez."

"Deputy." He turned back to Tom. "I'd prefer we talk alone."

"Phil and me, we don't have any secrets. Do we, Phil?"

"No sir."

"Sit down, Phil."

Sanchez sat.

Alonzo frowned. "Sheriff, I told you months ago that the

Whitfield case is closed. And now I learn that you're still running around, pestering people with questions."

Tom smiled. "I'm the Sheriff. That's what I do."

"You won't be Sheriff for long if —"

Tom raised his hand. "Hold on there, Peter. You sure you want to do that? Threaten me? In front of my deputy?"

Alonzo glanced at Sanchez, looked back at Tom. "Don't forget, Tom. There's an election in November."

"Managed to win without Carleton's money last time. Figure I can do it again."

"It may be that things've changed."

"Maybe so."

"Tom, just because you lost Carla —"

"Okay," said Tom. "I'm real tired of this. Dirt tired. Carla died by accident. She was moving one of my handguns, an automatic. It went off. If anyone was responsible for her dying, it was me. I shoulda kept the damn thing locked away. Not a single day goes by, not one, I don't think about that. But Carla didn't kill herself. She didn't have any reason to kill herself."

For a moment Alonzo stared at him. Finally he nodded. "All right. Fine, Tom. I just hope you know what you're doing."

"I know what I'm doing, Peter. Question is, what is it *you're* doing, exactly?"

Alonzo shook his head, glanced at Sanchez, and then turned and stalked from the room, slamming the door shut behind him.

Tom turned to Sanchez. "What was it you were saying?"

Sanchez shook his head. "Nothing, Tom. Doesn't matter. Why's Alonzo so hot to keep the case closed?"

"He owes Carleton. Like half the politicians in the party."

"Yeah, but how come Carleton wants to keep it closed?"

"Good question."

"Alonzo can make trouble for you, can't he?"

"Probably not as much as he thinks. Still a few folks out there who like the way I do business."

"So what happens now? Are you really going to pack it in?"

Tom smiled. "Just changed my mind."

"So what happens?"

"I keep leaning on people. Lois. Whitfield. Someone dies, you lean on the people made the money. Lean on them enough, maybe they break."

"Whitfield wasn't even in town."

"Lois was."

"She and Carleton both have alibis."

"Yeah. Handy."

"You really think Carleton was involved? He's a big man, Tom — a member of everything from the Rotary to the Gun Club. They say he's gonna run for county commissioner this year."

"Yeah. I heard that."

CHAPTER
TWENTY-EIGHT

Blue streamers of smoke swirled beneath the Cantina's brown-stained tin ceiling. The air was draped with the smells of cigarettes and cigars, sweat and perfume, and the room was crowded with the excited rumble of conversation, the bright bark of laughter.

Lois was as happy as she'd ever been. They were the center of the excitement, she and Raoul and Murray; they were the cause of it. It swirled around their little table simply because they were there, Raoul buying the drinks, Murray laughing, everyone in the room looking at the three of them with admiration and respect and maybe even a little awe.

"Patsy!" Raoul called out over the din.

Behind the bar, Patsy yelled back, "That's my name!"

"Another round," Raoul shouted. "For everyone!" He waved his hand in a circle over his head.

Sitting at the bar beside his cousin Pete, Esteban Morales whooped. Someone on the far side of the room applauded.

Lois looked at Raoul and he grinned at her, his dark brown eyes gleaming. He was happy as she was, as delighted to be here.

It still sometimes seemed impossible that she could be married to a man like him – handsome and smart, rich and famous, a man who'd been everywhere and done everything.

When he'd asked her, that very first day he came back, she was so surprised that she didn't know what to say. Finally, she came out with, "You're serious?"

He had been sitting on the bleachers, alongside the polo field, looking up at her. Tom Delgado had just driven away. Raoul's eyes were shiny.

"I'm serious," he said.

Looking down at him, she stroked his hair. "Why me, Sugar?"

He smiled, a sad smile that made her chest ache. "Because," he said, "we're made for each other, the two of us. You and I."

"You could have any woman you want. Any woman in the world."

"You're the one I want."

"Tell me why me."

"There's no pretense in you. No bullshit. You don't give a damn what anyone thinks or says."

She smiled. "Lot of people think that makes me some kind of bitch."

His mouth twitched. "Nothing wrong with being a bitch."

"Hey," she said.

His right hand was hooked on her hip. Still looking up at her, he slid the hand down along the outside of her skirt, down below her knee under her skirt and then up along the inside of her thigh, his knuckles sparking against her flesh. The hand scooped between her legs, and she felt the breath leave her, felt her body sag.

"Sugar," she sighed, and she cupped her hands over his, above the skirt, and swayed into his palm, into the spreading warmth. For a few seconds neither of them moved. Then she bent forward, kissed him, met the heat of his mouth. Their teeth clicked, their tongues rolled. She took her hands from his, wrapped her arms around his neck. His right hand moved, fingers sliding over her panties, sliding into them, the silk slick and damp now.

He touched her cheek with his left hand and drew back his head so he could look her in the eyes. "I need you," he said.

"You got me, Sugar," she said.

"So," he said. "Yes?"

"So yes, baby. Definitely."

"We'll have to wait for a while. Until everything's settled. Emily's business."

"Whenever you're ready," she said, and curled toward him again, cheek against cheek. She licked his ear. "Say it again," she whispered.

"What?" His left hand found her breast, his thumb creeping over her nipple, stiffening it.

"You need me," she said. "Say it."

"I need you," he said, and his voice was so tight that for a moment she thought he was angry. But then his mouth found hers and his right hand gripped at her, kneading, and she knew that everything was okay.

She pulled away. She was having trouble breathing. "Is there a bed around here someplace?"

They never made it to a bed that day. They made love on the sofa in the living room.

He hadn't been lying about needing her, not that day and not since.

Other men had wanted her, but no one had ever needed her the way Raoul did. He made love to her every night, once, twice, three times, his hands and his mouth roaming all over her, hungry, desperate.

It gave her a kind of power, and occasionally she tested its boundaries, trying to determine what those boundaries were, trying to determine who *they* were, she and Raoul.

They would be in the kitchen or the living room and she would look at him and say softly, "Come here, baby," and his eyes would go a bit lost, like the eyes of a man on drugs, and he would come to her, reaching out for her, and in a few minutes their clothes would be gone and they would be on the floor and his trembling hands would be stroking her, his lips sucking, his tongue sliding over her armpit, her belly, her back.

She could get warm just thinking about it. And now, looking at him beside her, she felt it again, that sultry slackness of flesh, and she wanted him, wanted him to want her, right now, right here in the middle of the noisy, chattering crowd. She laid her hand on his leg, above the knee, and squeezed it.

He smiled down at her, then reached out and gripped the back of her head and leaned forward and kissed her, long and hard.

"Please, children," said Murray. "You'll frighten the horses."

Raoul broke away, leaving his arm on her shoulders, and turned to him, grinning. "You're just jealous."

Murray smiled. "Envious," he said. "I haven't felt that way about anything since my parents gave me a model train set."

She laughed. "How old were you, Murray?"

"Thirty-four," he said.

And they laughed together, she and Raoul.

She asked Murray, "Are you really gonna run for county commissioner?"

"The party calls. I can only answer."

"How come I have a hard time seeing you as a politician?"

"A lack of imagination, my dear. I shall become the George Washington of San Miguel County. I shall —"

He stopped, staring toward the bar.

Lois turned, felt Raoul turn beside her.

Tom Delgado stood there, between Esteban Morales and Charlie Sutcliffe.

Like Murray, everyone sitting along the bar had stopped talking. They all knew about Delgado crashing the wedding party, and they all wanted to see what would happen next.

Raoul told Murray, "That Sheriff of yours is beginning to get on my nerves."

Lois turned to Murray, "This afternoon I was at Ilfield's and he was standing outside the whole time. When I went in and when I came out. He was just standing there, watching me."

"Did he say anything?" Murray asked. "Harass you?"

"No. Just stood there."

"Forget it, children. Let's blow this joint and go back to my place. I've got a surprise for you. Raoul, you remember Paris?"

Raoul frowned. "What about it?"

"It's the same sort of surprise."

"I'm a little tired, Murray."

"What surprise?" Lois asked them.

"We'll talk about it at my place," said Murray. "Shall we?"

To leave the bar, they had to pass Tom Delgado, who still stood there, a cup of coffee in front of him. Just before they did, Raoul handed a big wad of bills to Patsy without counting them, and he said, "Don't forget Inspector Javert, Patsy. He looks like he could use a drink."

"Who?" said Patsy.

"That'd be me," Delgado told her. He turned to Raoul. "No thanks, Mr. Whitfield. The coffee's fine. Lois, how you doing?"

"Just peachy, Tom."

"Glad to hear it."

"Shall we go?" said Murray.

"Come on, Lois," said Raoul.

138

"G'night, now," said Delgado, and turned back to his coffee.

Lois stared at him. Why was he being such a bastard?

He turned back to her. "Help you, Lois?"

"Come on, Lois," said Raoul, and stroked her arm.

"Good night, Tom," she said.

He smiled at her. "Night, Lois."

The three of them went to Murray's house. It turned into a very interesting night.

CHAPTER
TWENTY-NINE

Raoul woke up with pain poised like a knife blade at the back of his head, just behind his right ear. His stomach was sour, his lungs were clogged and cramped. Clearing his throat, he looked at the clock on the nightstand. Ten fifteen.

Sunlight was spilling into the room. They had forgotten to draw the curtains last night.

He smiled. Their performance on the bed, and across it, and beside it, had probably been a huge eye-opener for anyone passing by the window.

He turned and looked at Lois. She lay on her side beneath the sheet, facing him, her mouth slightly parted, her small hand balled against her chin. Her lipstick was blurred, her mascara smudged, and she seemed as vulnerable and fragile as a child.

She was, he decided once again, simply the best thing that had ever happened to him. It was a cliché, of course, but in a way she had given him back his youth. She had brought back a passion he had thought forever lost. Sometimes, shuddering as he sank into her arms, he simply disappeared, vanished in a kind of delicious surrender.

He remembered thinking, when he arrived back in town on the train, that he should avoid her. But as soon as Murray had driven him to her house that morning, and he had seen her again, her shiny black hair, her big black glistening eyes, he realized how wrong he had been. She was the one good thing that had come out of the whole sad sorry mess.

She was funny and smart and brave. She was passionate. She was enthusiastic. She was open to anything.

Sometimes too open.

But she was young and she was hungry for experience. The important thing, the only genuinely important thing, was that she was as crazy about him as he was about her.

Everything was perfect now. All he had to do was start working again. Start facing that blank page.

Soon. After all he'd been through, he needed some time for himself and Lois. In a way, the two of them were still on their honeymoon. As soon as things settled down, he'd get back to the grind.

He tossed aside the sheet, rolled off the bed, and padded over to the window.

Another splendid day, the sky blue, the air—

An old Dodge police car was parked in the drive, just beyond the polo field. Delgado.

Raoul snatched his robe off the chair, tugged it on, and stalked from the bedroom, down the hallway, across the living room to the telephone. He grabbed the earpiece, viciously wound the crank. When the operator came on, he snapped out Murray's office number. The phone rang.

Murray's secretary answered and put him through.

"Murray Carleton."

"Murray, he's out there again."

"Good morning, dear boy."

"He's out there again."

"I did catch that."

"It's the third time this month, Murray."

"What more can I do? I've already spoken with Alonzo."

"Isn't this harassment? Can't we get some kind of restraining order?"

"He's the sheriff. You can't restrain the sheriff. But look, Raoul. The elections are next month. He'll be out."

"And what'll we do in the meantime?"

"Why not take off? Leave town. By the time you get back, this'll all be over."

"Where should I go?"

"Anywhere you want. Anywhere in the world. For God's sake, Raoul, you've got the money."

• • •

141

He walked across the bedroom floor, sat down on the bed. Gently, he brushed the hair from her forehead.

"Hey," he said. "Kiddo?"

She closed her mouth, swallowed, made chewing motions.

"Kiddo?"

She rolled slowly onto her back, opened her eyes, slipped her arm from beneath the sheet. Smiling, she put her hand on his shoulder. "Morning, Sugar."

"How'd you like to leave town for a while?"

"Huh?"

"Travel. See everything you've always wanted to see."

She closed her eyes and smiled. "Paris?" she said. "I always did want to see Paris."

"Why bother with Paris? What about Rome? Athens, Cairo, Shanghai?"

Her eyes opened. "You're serious?"

The same question she had asked him months ago, alongside the polo field.

He grinned. "I'm serious."

"Do I get my pick?"

"Why pick? Why not all of them? And Nairobi, Capetown, Rio."

"Hey. Really?"

"By the time we get back, Delgado will be gone."

"How do you know that?"

"Murray. He says the Sheriff won't be re-elected."

"How does Murray know?"

He smiled down at her. "Murray knows all, sees all."

"When would we go?"

"What about today?"

She laughed. "You're nuts."

"We can take the afternoon train down to Albuquerque. Fly to L.A. tomorrow. Get a boat for Hawaii."

Her hand tightened on his shoulder. "Really?"

"Really. We can start getting ready right now."

She laughed again. "Not right now." She pulled at him. "Come here, baby."

CHAPTER THIRTY

It was one amazement after the other.

They traveled first class all the way, people waiting on them hand and foot.

They saw Honolulu, Tokyo, Kyoto, Hong Kong, Saigon, Bangkok, Mandalay, Calcutta, Bombay, Nairobi, Khartoum, Cairo, Constantinople, Athens, Rome, Venice, Prague, Vienna, Berlin, Amsterdam, London and a half a million other places. They rode horses in Kashmir, elephants in Siam, camels in the Sudan. They sailed on a dhow from Mombasa to Lamu, on a caique from Karpathos to Rhodes. They took trains through the Sahara, the Anatolian Plains, the Alps.

And the meals! Steak and lobster and goose liver and caviar, absinthe and Champagne and ouzo and cognac and single malt scotch.

Everywhere they stopped, they bought something gorgeous and Raoul paid to have it shipped back to Dead Horse. A jade bowl, a Ming vase, an ivory Buddha, a set of ebony tribal masks, a flocatti rug, a gold alarm clock, a matching pair of vicuna coats.

Occasionally she got a bit tired of traveling, a bit bored with foreigners, even a bit homesick, but Raoul always found something fun to do. In Shanghai they smoked opium; in Morocco, kif from a water pipe. They were in Zurich in April, and he bought her, for her birthday, her exact weight in chocolates, one hundred and ten pounds. They left almost all of it behind for the maids in the hotel.

From London they took a boat to Lisbon, and then another boat across the Atlantic to Rio. She saw dolphins and flying fish and once, off in the hazy distance, a whale. In Brazil they ate shrimp all the way up the coast, from Rio to Salvador to Recife, until she was practically sick of the stuff. In Bogota they tried cocaine; in Havana, heroin.

It took them over a year, and when they returned to L.A., Raoul bought them matching Cord automobiles, convertibles. She didn't know a thing about driving, so Raoul hired a man to bring one of the cars back, and they drove the other to New Mexico together, through California and Arizona along Route 66. Along the way, he taught her how to drive.

They got back to Las Vegas in May of 1936.

CHAPTER
THIRTY-ONE

Tom was sitting back, reading the newspaper, when Phil Sanchez knocked at the open door. He looked up.

"Did you hear?" said Sanchez. "They're back."

"Who?"

"Whitfield and Lois."

Tom folded the newspaper. "When?"

"Yesterday. I talked to Bob Gomez, over at the County Clerk's Office. Murray Carleton set it up for a chunk of Dead Horse to get sold. A hundred acres, over toward the Pecos. Whitfield came in this morning to sign the papers."

Tom stood up and laid the paper on his desk. "Guess I'll head on out there and say hello."

"How come he's selling property, Tom? I thought he got a big piece of money from the wife."

"I'll ask him."

• • •

At the ranch, two tractors were rumbling and puffing as they towed mower reels across the polo field. The green smell of fresh-cut grass floated along the air.

He parked the Dodge beside Murray Carleton's Packard. There were two other cars there, a pair of those new Cord convertibles, long and sleek and black, maybe the most beautiful cars Tom had ever seen. Just one of them would cost more than he made in a year.

He went through the gate, across the lawn, and across the portal to the front door. He knocked.

Whitfield opened the door in a pair of jeans, barefoot and bare-chested. His hair was messy and his cheeks were stubbled. He frowned. "Inspector Javert," he said. "You don't give up, do you?"

Tom smiled. "Supposed to be a good thing in a sheriff. Just came out to welcome you back."

Lois, in a black night gown, slipped up behind Raoul, put her hand on his shoulder. "What is it, Sugar?" She saw Tom. "Oh fuck."

Raoul turned aside, coughed, turned back to Tom. "My lawyer's here, Delgado."

"Got a cold?"

"Tom," said Lois, "why don't you just leave us alone."

He turned to Whitfield. "Heard you sold off some property, Mr. Whitfield. Money starting to run out?"

"All right," said Murray Carleton. He wore slacks, a white shirt with its sleeves rolled up. His striped tie was unknotted, his collar open. Protectively, he stepped in front of Whitfield and Lois. "That's enough. You're on private property, Sheriff."

"You keep saying that."

"Do you have a warrant?"

"Nope."

"Then I'm going to have to ask you to leave. Otherwise, I'll be informing —"

"Yeah. The District Attorney. You already tried that. Didn't work too well. Tried to run me out of office, too, and that didn't work either. I hear you belong to the Gun Club. Maybe you could just shoot me."

Carleton smiled. "Or I could talk to the Governor. I know him fairly well."

"Sure. Why not."

"Goodbye, Sheriff."

"Gotta admit, though, the three of you make for a nice picture."

Carleton shut the door.

CHAPTER
THIRTY-TWO

The polo field was immaculate, bright green under a cloudless sky. From their bench on the bleachers, in the shade of the big piñon, Lois looked out across the expanse of grass and she felt a hollowness inside her. "No one's gonna come," she said.

"They'll come," he said, and cleared his throat.

She rubbed his arm. "You gotta quit smoking, Sugar."

He took a sip of bourbon.

Overhead, the white canopy snapped in the breeze. To their right was another snapping canopy, and beneath it, behind the bar, sat Patsy from the Cantina, reading a copy of *Silver Screen* magazine.

They heard the sound of an automobile.

Murray Carleton's big Packard came slowly down the road, towing a silver horse trailer. Under the other canopy, Patsy stood up and set aside her magazine.

The car stopped about fifty feet away and Murray stepped out. In a white short-sleeved shirt, and white pants ballooning out above a pair shiny black boots, he sauntered across the lawn.

"Where is everyone?" he asked Raoul.

"We *are* everyone," said Raoul.

"No one's coming, Murray," she said.

Murray looked out at the empty field. "Ah, well," he said. He smiled at Raoul. "Screw 'em." He tapped his pants pocket. "Magic Dust. Let's go inside and play for a while."

"Patsy," said Raoul, nodding toward the other canopy. "I've got to send her home."

"Not necessarily," said Murray. "Is she discreet? She's got a perky little mouth."

Lois stood up and walked away.

She heard Raoul call out for her, but it was the sound of someone in a dream, dim and distant. She could feel her feet slapping against the ground, but she seemed to be floating over it. She aimed herself at the car, the big black Cord parked beside Raoul's. She yanked open the door, threw herself inside, tugged the door shut. As always, the key was in the ignition. She turned it and the powerful V-8 engine came growling alive.

She glanced in the side mirror, saw Raoul stalking toward her. Putting the car in reverse, she spun the wheel and hit the gas. Gravel pinged against the undercarriage. She shoved the stick into first and slammed her foot on the gas pedal. The front tires bit into the dirt and the car lunged forward. She shoved the shift into second, and then into third.

She could head for the highway or she could turn left and stay on the dirt road that circled Dead Horse. For a moment she wanted the highway, wanted to roar out onto Route 66 west and stay on it, the wind tearing at her hair, until she reached California and the coast.

She had no money, no clothes but the dress she was wearing.

She would find someone. She would get a job somewhere. She'd always been able to find someone, always been able to get a job.

She didn't know anyone out there.

She didn't have the strength to start over again.

Downshifting, she spun the steering wheel to the left, floored the gas pedal. The car swayed as it made the turn, and she shifted into third.

Bouncing in the seat, she peered into the rear view mirror. All she could see was a dull billowing wall of red dust.

She squinted into the side mirror, and she could see the other Cord, back beyond the dust.

She knew the road. She and Raoul had chased after each other on it, him in his car, she in hers. It had been fun then, the two of them playing at cops and robbers. Now all she wanted to do was drive and drive and drive, drive in endless circles, punish the big beautiful car, punish Raoul, punish herself.

She sped past the windmill and the stock tank, took the next long sweeping curve at fifty miles an hour. She downshifted for the upcoming right turn, swung through it, and then floored the pedal. The car went rocketing into the straight, drumming as it raced over the road's washboarding. Another left curve was approaching, and she braked, slowed, then gave the car some gas.

But the tires slid free, rightward, and she braked again and went into a skid, the car beginning to drift sideways. She took her foot off the brake and counter-steered, just as Raoul had taught her, but it was no good, and suddenly the car was careening over uneven ground, tires thumping, brush and grasses snapping against the metalwork. Her teeth clacked.

A small piñon tree was directly ahead, and she froze.

The car's bumper slammed into the tree, branches snapping, brittle pine cones flying as the engine stalled out. She flopped forward, rag doll, and her head smacked against the steering wheel. She bounced back against the seat, her neck whipping. Slumped there, she felt something trickle vaguely down her face.

The door opened.

"Lois! Jesus Christ!"

Raoul.

He was stroking her forehead with his handkerchief — he always carried a handkerchief, a gentleman always did — and he was saying, "Are you okay? Kiddo, can you hear me?"

She pushed his hand away. "Lemme out."

"Here. I'll help you."

"Go 'way."

He stood back and she pulled herself out of the car. She wavered for a moment, then leaned back against the car's side, her arms dangling, her head hanging. Her brand new black pumps were filmed with dust. As she looked, a small star of bright red suddenly splotched onto the leather. Blood.

"Jesus Christ, Lois," he said. "You scared the shit out of me."

She took a deep breath and then all at once she was crying.

"Lois," he said. "Kiddo."

She felt his arms go around her, and at first she resisted, but then she sagged against him, the sobs wracking her.

"Kiddo," he said. He stroked her back. "Kiddo."

"Shit," she said, and buried her face in his neck.

149

"It's okay. It's okay."

"Jesus, Raoul, what's gonna happen to us?"

His arms tightened. "We'll be fine, kiddo. We'll be fine."

Off in the distance, the wind blew through the pines.

BOOK THREE
1941

CHAPTER
THIRTY-THREE

Over the next few years, Tom drove out to Dead Horse only occasionally, once every few months. Sitting there in his new Dodge – a gift from the County – he would stare out across the polo field at the ranch house and wonder what was happening inside. What was their life like, Whitfield's and Lois's?

He knew some of it. Everyone in town kept telling him.

The two of them got loud drunk at the Cantina, and Patsy had to ask them to leave. They had a fight with each other in Ilfield's Department Store. They took a trip to Los Angeles, and then another to Hot Springs, Arkansas. They got raucous again in the Cantina. But a few nights later they were back in the bar, snuggling up to each other.

That was the outside, the public side. What happened to them in private? What did they talk about? What did they do?

Whatever it was, he knew that it was none of his business.

But it still rankled him, every day, to think about them living out there on Emily Whitfield's ranch, going through Emily Whitfield's money.

Maybe he should just let go, forget about them. Forget about Emily Whitfield.

But he kept seeing her as he had seen her that long-ago Fourth of July. Handing that cotton candy to young Emily. Her hair fluttering in the breeze, her face alight with happiness.

151

Always, afterward, when Tom drove back to town, he was depressed.

Jane Templeton called at least once a year, usually around Christmastime, and each time he told her he had nothing to tell her.

Murray Carleton was appointed by the Governor to head a Commission on Corruption in State Government. Appropriate, Tom thought. Everyone kept saying that Carleton would be Governor himself one day. Probably after the next election, in '44.

Maria got her dog, a spaniel puppy she named Carmen because it whined and howled all the time, and she thought that was very operatic. She had stopped using the swing set – it had become, for her, an antique. Tom knew he should unbolt the damn thing and tear it down, but he couldn't bring himself to start.

Whitfield kept selling off pieces of Dead Horse. He sold some of Emily Whitfield's art, too, and he sold the two Cord automobiles.

CHAPTER
THIRTY-FOUR

Lois woke up and looked across the bed. Raoul was gone. She looked at the golden alarm clock. Eleven o'clock.

She swung her legs off the bed, bent over to pick up her robe from the floor. Standing, she slipped on the robe, tied the belt. She walked to the door, pulled it open, padded down the hallway.

Raoul sat on the living room sofa in his bathrobe, hunched forward, his elbows on his knee, a drink in his hand. He was staring at the coffee table. On it were the remains of last night. A half-empty bottle of Calvados. Her empty glass, lipstick on the rim. Murray's glass, still holding an inch of liquor. The mirror and the razor blade.

She sat down beside him. "Drinking already, Sugar?"

Without looking at her, he said, "It's all over."

"What is?"

He looked at her, looked back at the coffee table. "Murray told me last night. After you went to bed. It's all over."

"What do you mean?"

He sat there, staring forward. "The money. It's gone. All of it."

She frowned. "What happened to it?"

"We ate it. Drank it." He glanced at the mirror. "It's gone."

"Yeah, but…. Can't you write one of your books?"

He smiled bleakly. "It's been a while."

"Hey. It'll come back to you, Sugar. If you did it before, you can do it again."

He shook his head. "You don't get it. There's nothing left. Not the ranch, not the money. Not me."

She moved closer to him, took his arm. "We can start again.

Together. We can move. California. Los Angeles. You've got friends there. Movie people. You told me."

He turned to her. "Friends. Right. Like our friends here."

"We've got plenty of friends. All those people at the Cantina."

He turned to the coffee table.

"We can do it, Sugar," she said.

Another bleak smile. "Sure," he said.

CHAPTER
THIRTY-FIVE

One April morning, Tom's telephone rang. He picked it up.
"Sheriff Delgado."

"Sheriff? Wally Brown, at the station."

"Morning, Wally. What can I do for you?"

"You hear about Raoul Whitfield?"

"Hear what?"

"Hear he's leaving Dead Horse?"

"How do we know that, Wally?"

"My cousin. Terrell?"

"Yeah."

"He works for O'Reilly's. The moving van company?"

"Right."

"He was out there yesterday, loading up stuff for Whitfield. Wasn't that much left, he said. But he emptied out the house."

"Where's it all going?"

"Right here in town. To Murray Carleton's place."

"And where's Whitfield going?"

"California. Him and Lois. Least, that's what he told Terrell."

"When?"

"When are they leaving, you mean?"

"Yeah, Wally."

"Today, he said. He said he was leaving today."

• • •

The polo field hadn't been mowed or watered for months, maybe years. The grass was long and scraggly, overgrown with weeds.

Overhead, to the north, the sky was gray. A storm was coming.

Tom saw that Emily Whitfield's Cadillac was parked by the front gate, its rear doors open. The rear seat was stuffed with cardboard boxes, and Whitfield and Lois had been tying more of them to its roof. They stood on opposite sides of the vehicle and watched him as he parked the Dodge.

He got out, walked toward the Cadillac. Whitfield was on the car's near side. He was pale and he looked tired, but he was wearing freshly pressed brown slacks and a white silk shirt, a pair of two-toned shoes.

"Heard you were leaving," Tom said.

"That must've made your day," said Whitfield.

"Not especially."

Lois had been circling around the Cadillac. Now she came to Whitfield and put her arm through his, leaned against him. She wore a black skirt, a pale yellow blouse.

"Why not?" she asked Tom. "You got what you want. We're leaving town."

"That's not what I want."

"What do you want?"

"The truth. About Emily Whitfield. About that night."

"We told you the truth. We weren't here then, neither one of us."

"Sheriff," said Whitfield, and then turned to one side and coughed into his fist.

"Doesn't sound too good," Tom said. "Maybe you should get that looked at."

Whitfield cleared his throat. "Sheriff," he said, "suppose you've been wrong all along. Suppose Emily did kill herself."

"Yeah?"

"How would you feel? You've pestered us. You've harassed us. You've turned our friends against us. And now you've forced us to leave our own home."

"Don't figure it that way. Wasn't me spent her money. Wasn't me sold her ranch, piece by piece. Wasn't me drank it all away."

Lois said, "You wouldn't leave us alone!"

Tom nodded. "Well, that's all over now. You can go off to California."

156

"Fuck you, Tom," she said. She turned to Raoul. "Come on, Sugar. Let's finish up."

"You go ahead," Whitfield told her. "I'll be right in."

She glanced at Tom, then spun about and strode off around the car, through the gate, toward the house.

Whitfield looked at Tom. "What if you've been wrong, Sheriff? What if you've been wrong all this time?"

"I figure I can live with it." He looked up at the sky, looked back at Whitfield. "Better get a move on. Looks like a storm coming in."

"I loved my wife," said Whitfield. "I loved Emily."

"Good for you."

Whitfield smiled. It was a charming smile, open and radiant, the smile of a younger and happier man. For a moment he was no longer worn and pale, and Tom understood what he must have looked like in Paris, all those years ago.

"Fuck you, Tom," he said.

Tom nodded. "See you," he said, and turned and walked away.

Behind him, he heard Whitfield call out, "I doubt it."

157

CHAPTER
THIRTY-SIX

When Jane Templeton called that Christmas, Tom told her that Whitfield and Lois had left for California.

She said, "Is there any way to learn what they're doing out there?"

"What would be the point, Ma'am?"

"Well…. Yes. Yes, I suppose I'm just being silly. It's over, isn't it, Sheriff?"

"Afraid so."

Whitfield and Lois were gone. Victor Chervet was gone. Pablo Ramirez, one of the two Dead Horse ranch hands, had enlisted in the Marine Corps. Johnny Archuleta, the other, had gotten shot and killed one night in Santa Fe. Tom had gone down there, on the off chance that there was some connection to Mrs. Whitfield's death, but the local police were sure that the killing was some kind of gang situation.

And Murray Carleton was probably going to be the next governor of New Mexico.

"I'm sorry, Sheriff," Miss Templeton said.

"Yes, Ma'am. Me too."

"But if something does turn up…."

"I'll for sure let you know."

"And if anything does…if you ever need any help with it — money, whatever — I hope you'll ask me."

"Don't think the situation'll come up, Ma'am. But I thank you."

"I know some people in Los Angeles. I think they'd be willing to help, too."

"Yes, Ma'am. Thank you. How's the girl? Little Emily?"

"She's fine. And how's Maria?"

"Just fine, thanks. Still getting straight A's."

"Good. Well, I should go. I hope you have a good Christmas, Sheriff, and a happy new year."

"Thank you ma'am. Same to you."

Tom hung up and sat back.

Someone had killed Emily Whitfield and gotten away with it. Probably no one would ever know who that someone might be. Tom didn't like it, but there it was.

1943

CHAPTER
THIRTY-SEVEN

From where she sat on the parapet, her feet dangling some fifteen stories above the street, she could see across the rooftops and out over the water. The Golden Gate Bridge spanned the bay to the west, blood red against the dark blue of the water and the paler blue of sky.

It was a perfect day. No fog, no rain, the air so clear that she could see the tiny houses scattered up and down the green hills of Marin County.

She looked off, toward the Pacific. Men were dying out there now, American soldiers dying pointlessly on the beaches of tiny, barren, useless islands.

She remembered the beaches of Thailand and India, the eight mile sweep of golden sand on Lamu, in Kenya.

That trip had been one perfect day after another. Throughout it all, she had told herself that she had to remember this specific place, that specific thing – the sweet salty taste of grilled octopus, the fragrance of frangipani, the humming silence of the old Kyoto temple, the view from the soaring height of Sugar Loaf in Rio. She had tucked all those moments away like a miser hoarding gold, so that one day she could slip them out, one by one, and marvel at them. Things might never be this good again – she had actually thought that, many times during the journey – and it would be so lovely to have the memories, to remind her of how happy the two of them had been.

Memory, she had learned, doesn't work that way. The past

doesn't enrich the present — it only throws the emptiness into relief. Every memory becomes a burden, a bitter reminder of better days.

But she had nothing left now, except the past, and she couldn't stop herself from remembering.

The way he had come into the bar that very first night, so beautiful and sleek and sad. Those fumbling moments in the back of his Lincoln, hot skin sliding over hot skin. His laughter when he came back to her from L.A. His shining eyes when he asked her to marry him. The two of them at the wedding, everything wild and wonderful, all her friends gathered together on the bright green grass of Dead Horse. Those long laughing nights at the Cantina

Now he was lost to her, and her own earlier self was lost to her, and every day the pain grew worse, the memories grew heavier. Liquor didn't help. Drugs didn't help. Men didn't help. Nothing helped.

She looked out across the bay. Green hills, so far away across the flat blue water. Tiny houses. Who lived in them? Who were those people? Had their lives spiraled down to endless repetitions of the same empty endless day?

It began in the morning and it continued, relentless, until she sagged back into bed. Taking a shower, brushing her teeth, putting on make-up, going to work, forcing a smile — everything she did was exactly the same, hollow and meaningless, day after day after day.

She took a breath.

Say it, she heard herself say.

I need you.

She didn't jump exactly. From her seat on the parapet, all she had to do was let herself go.

161

CHAPTER
THIRTY-EIGHT

The War dragged on, in Europe and the South Pacific. Phil Sanchez wanted to enlist, but Tom persuaded him that he'd be just as useful here in San Miguel County as he would in North Africa or Sicily or the Marshall Islands.

Maria was attending the University of New Mexico down in Albuquerque. Tom had wanted her to stay in town and attend Highlands, the local branch of the state system, but naturally she was determined to be on her own. Tom was left with Carmen, the spaniel, who had been around six years now and who still hadn't shown a single sign of intelligence.

Jane Templeton still called, once a year, at Christmastime, but they mostly just chatted about what each of them had been doing..

On a Friday in July, Tom was on the telephone, talking to Hector Garcia, one of the new deputies. There had been a car wreck at Tomas De Baca's place, south of town. No one had been hurt, but Tomas's front fence had been smashed, and Hector figured it would take a while to calm him down. He wanted to shoot the driver.

Someone knocked at Tom's door. "Can you handle it, Hector?" he asked.

"Yes, sir."

"Any problems, call me back."

"Yes, sir."

"Okay." He hung up and turned to the door. "Come on in."

It was Phil Sanchez, holding a copy of the local newspaper. Crossing the room, he raised it. "You see this?"

The headline said "CARLETON SAYS HE WILL RUN."

"No big surprise there," said Tom.

"No. Inside."

Sanchez opened the paper, leafed through it, found the page he wanted, and folded the paper back. He handed it to Tom.

Tom read. "Shit," he said.

"Says she committed suicide," said Sanchez. "Out there in San Francisco."

"Yeah."

"You figure maybe Whitfield gave her a hand?"

"Guess I better find out."

CHAPTER
THIRTY-NINE

H e's been here for nearly two years now," said the Veterans'
Hospital nurse. "Right this way, Mr. Delgado."

In her fifties, too plump for her white uniform, she led Tom
into an open ward.

It had high white ceilings and white walls. There were white
screens set up along the floor on both sides, one after another,
running down to the far end of the room. On the left wall, tall
opened windows let in the sunlight. White lace curtains at their
edges bellied out as the wind wafted in.

The room had a ghostly, dreamlike feel. But, despite the breeze,
the air was tainted with the smell of carbolic and rotting meat
and loose bowels.

As Tom followed the nurse, he glanced between the screens.

Men lay there on cots, gaunt and pale. Some were coughing;
some were asleep. Some simply stared up at the ceiling.

"He was terribly upset when he heard about Mrs. Whitfield,"
said the nurse. "She was up in San Francisco, you know. She
hadn't come down here for a while, but she wrote to him nearly
every week. Here we are. Raoul?"

If the nurse hadn't told him, Tom wouldn't have known who
the man was.

His face was almost fleshless, eaten from within. His chest
seemed flattened, as though it had collapsed. His eyes, closed
now, had sunk back into their sockets. Resting above the covers,
down at his sides, his limp speckled hands were bony, the veins
standing out like snarls of blue twine.

"Raoul?" said the nurse. "Look, dear. We have company."

Whitfield opened his eyes, took in the nurse, looked over at

Tom. After a moment, he smiled faintly. "Javert. Welcome to Pasadena."

Tom turned to the nurse. "Thank you, Ma'am."

"I thought you said Delgado," she said.

"A joke we have."

She nodded. "Try not to tire him out," she said. She looked at Raoul and smiled brightly. "We need our rest, don't we, dear?"

Still faintly smiling, Whitfield was staring up at Tom.

"I'll leave you then," said the nurse to Tom, and she turned and walked back toward the entrance.

On far side of the cot, against the wall, was a small night stand. On the near side, facing the cot, was a slatted wooden chair.

Tom sat down in the chair. "Heard about Lois," he said.

Whitfield nodded. "And you came out to give me your condolences."

"I came out—"

Raoul raised his frail right hand. "You came out because you thought, 'I've got the bastard now.'"

"Something like that," Tom admitted

"Sorry to disappoint you. San Francisco is a bit out of my territory. I can barely make it to the toilet these days."

Tom nodded. "I talked to your doctor."

"Portman? You got all the juicy details?"

"TB, he said."

"And the liver. And the heart's not much good either." Again, faintly, he smiled. "But there are those who say it never was."

Tom said nothing.

"Did Portman tell you the prognosis?" Whitfield asked him.

"He said not to be optimistic."

Whitfield laughed, a dry brittle cackle that became a cough. He rolled his head to the side until he was finished, then rolled it back to look at Tom. He swallowed. "He didn't know to whom he spoke, did he, Javert? You have every reason for optimism. I may last one more year. Two, if I'm lucky. If you call that luck."

"Maybe it's time to talk."

"The death bed confessional? Tie up all those loose ends, patch up all those pesky holes in the plot?" He shook his head. "Hack

165

work stuff." He swallowed again. "Lois didn't leave a note, they said."

"No. Not much doubt about it, though. People saw her going up to the roof."

"She worked the elevator in that hotel. Did you know that?"

Tom nodded. "I talked to the police down there."

"I'll bet you did." He cleared his throat. "You know, she wrote to me once and she told me that every day, every single day, someone said to her, 'Get a lot of ups and downs in this business.' She heard that every day."

"Old joke."

"If I heard that every day, that same stupid line, sooner or later I'd jump off the roof myself." He smiled, but the smile faded and he looked up at the ceiling.

Leaning forward, Tom put his forearms along his thighs, clasped his hands together. "For a while there," he said, "you had the world by the tail. You had it all. Money, a ranch, a beautiful wife. You could do anything, be anything. You nearly lost it, you came damn close to losing it, but you got it back. All of it. The money. The ranch. Another beautiful wife. World by the tail."

Whitfield still stared at the ceiling.

"And what've you got now?" Tom asked him. "Both your women are dead. The money's gone. You're lying here with holes in your lungs and a liver that's turning into cement."

Whitfield's glance flicked down to him. "Nice way with a phrase. Who'd have thought?"

"Remember Emily's daughter? Little Emily? She still thinks her mother committed suicide. Thinks her mother couldn't even wait a couple of months to see her."

"She's not my daughter. I'm not responsible for her."

"You never been responsible for anyone in your whole life. Not even yourself."

"Do you get many compliments on your bedside manner?"

"Listen to me. All I want is the truth."

"What makes you think I have it?"

"Someone does."

"Not necessarily me."

"You're the obvious choice."

"Too obvious. What you want is the unlikely suspect."

"Stop playing games."

"They're all I have left, *mon Capitain.*"

Tom looked down for a moment, looked back up. "Listen. No matter what you arranged, no matter who you paid off, you're not going to jail. Not now. Not the way you are."

"Jail would be an improvement."

"You have my word. The only one I'll talk to is the girl. Think about her, Raoul. Think about —"

"Raoul. Are we buddies now? Are we buckaroos?"

"Think about what she's carrying. What she's been carrying. You can free her from that. You can free yourself."

Another smile. "Freedom. An elusive concept. And how do you know I won't invent something interesting, just to get you off my back? That's what I do for a living. Invent things. Sorry. What I used to do."

"All I want is the truth."

"How'd you get out here, Javert? San Miguel County didn't pay for your train ticket."

"I borrowed the money."

"Relentless, unstoppable."

"The girl," said Tom.

Whitfield looked up at the ceiling again. Tom waited. Somewhere in the ward, someone coughed.

The moment grew longer. Tom didn't move. He felt as though he were watching one of those stop-motion movies of a flower opening. He was afraid that if he did anything now, said anything, the film would stutter in the projector, blur out, and then burst into flame, disappearing forever.

At last Whitfield looked at him.

"I'll say this once," he said. "To you. And I'll never repeat it."

Tom nodded.

"I was in Los Angeles. I'm a pilot. I knew people who owned airplanes."

"Shit," said Tom, and sat back in the chair.

"What?"

"You flew out there and you landed on that goddamned polo field, didn't you? Shit."

"You're getting ahead of yourself, Sheriff."

"You went out there yourself, to kill her."

167

"Oh, for Christ's sake. Stop being the Stupid Cop. That was the last thing in the world I wanted. I wanted us to be together again. I wanted Emily. I tell this my way or not at all."

Tom nodded. "Go ahead. Tell it."

"I borrowed an airplane. A Lockheed Vega. The same plane Amelia Erhardt flew across the Atlantic. 450 horsepower Wasp engine. Cruising speed of 155 miles an hour. Range of over fifteen hundred miles. I left L.A. at about five in the afternoon, got to the ranch before midnight. The moon was nearly full."

"You followed the road. Route 66. It goes right by Dead Horse."

"I followed the road."

"I'm an idiot. The polo field. There must've been tracks. Where you landed."

"I had them mowed away as soon as I could."

Again, Tom nodded. "Go ahead."

CHAPTER FORTY

Far beneath him, in the moonlight, the road was a crisp black ribbon winding through the smudged gray countryside. Overhead, stars flickered.

He remembered Paris and that earlier flight, years ago.

The soaring Eiffel Tower, the Seine darkly glittering below. Emily's gleeful cry in his headphones when he looped the Fokker. Then the long dreamy float over the French landscape, coming up on Auxerre just as the sun rose. And then the picnic, the wine and cheese, the laughter, Emily's mouth beneath his, a whole new world opening up to him....

He had flown over Santa Fe less than half an hour ago. Dead Horse should be close.

There. Yes.

Slowly, banking the plane to the left, he circled the ranch.

He doubted that Emily had kept the grass of the polo field watered and cut. But he knew that the ground was level. ("We don't want the horses stumbling all over each other, like Keystone Kops.")

He came in low, from the west, keeping just above the scrub brush, and he throttled back into a glide. He kept the nose up as the main gear touched down on the grass, bounced lightly once, and then touched down again. He felt the rear gear settle in, and gently he hit the brakes. The Vega bumbled along for a couple hundred yards and then rolled to a stop. He shut off the engine and reached into his jacket, took out the pint of Jim Beam. He uncapped it and swallowed some bourbon.

Now. Emily.

• • •

He used his own key to let himself in. The house was still and dark, but he could see a strip of light at the bottom of the bedroom door. He walked past the guest room to the door. Inside, a radio was playing. He turned the knob, opened the door, stepped in.

Propped against the pillows, a drink in her right hand, a book in her lap, she was lying on the bed, above the covers. She turned to him, expressionless, and set the drink on the night stand . "Get out," she said flatly.

He pulled the door shut. "I only want to talk, Em," he said. "We need to talk."

"Get out of my house."

He moved toward her. "Em, it's not too late."

She tossed aside the book, swung her feet off the bed, lurched up from the mattress. She wavered for a moment, unsteady, and then wheeled to face him. Her face red now, she jabbed her finger toward the door. "Out!"

"Emily, please. I came all this way, just so we could talk. I flew all the way out here. Doesn't that mean anything to you?"

She stepped to the dresser, ripped open the top drawer, jerked out a big chrome-plated revolver. The Colt. He had given it to her when they first moved in.

Holding it in both hands, she aimed it at him. Her eyes were so narrow he couldn't see their color. "Get. Out."

He began to circle the bed, coming toward her. "Emily. I love you. I've always loved you."

"Liar. Liar! The only thing you ever loved was you. You and your damned writing. And you betrayed that, too, didn't you? Just like you betrayed me. Just like you betrayed Prudence. You got too comfortable, didn't you? Too rich and fat and comfortable to face a blank sheet of paper."

He came closer. She stood only three or four feet away.

Using both thumbs, she cocked the big pistol. The barrel wobbled.

He stopped. "Em, please. Put down the gun."

"You lost your courage. And you blamed me for it. That's why you picked up that stupid little slut, isn't it?"

"Em, remember how it used to be? Remember Paris? Remember how it was for us? It can be that way again."

170

"Is she impressed with the famous writer? Have you told her you haven't written a fucking word in years? That you'll never write —"

Raoul leaped forward and snatched at the pistol. Her left fist pounded at his face, and then she doubled over and swung away, trying to keep the gun from him. His fingers pried at her hand.

"Emily, I love —"

The pistol went off, the sound muffled by her body. He heard her sigh, and then she slumped to the bed, the gun still in her hand. Her eyes were open, startled.

"Emily," he said. "Em?"

She turned to him and took a deep shuddering breath. Her lips moved, as though she wanted to say something. And then, as she exhaled, her breathing stopped.

"Em," he said.

The door burst open. Victor Chervet stood there, staring at the body.

"It was an accident," Raoul told him.

Victor crossed himself.

"It was an accident," Raoul repeated. He stepped forward and touched her forehead.

"The police?" said Victor. "I call them?"

Raoul turned to him. "They won't believe it." He looked down again at Emily. "No. I've got to get out of here."

"Raoul...."

"I need your help, Victor. I need gas. I've got a plane. I need to refuel it."

"But —"

"Victor, you owe me. This was an accident. An accident."

He swung Emily's legs up onto the bed, lifted the pistol from her hand, wiped the fingerprints from it, stuck the weapon back in her hand. He turned to Victor. "I need your help. The gas in the barn. The tanks for the tractors."

"Yes," said Victor, and nodded. "Yes."

"You find her in the morning. When you bring in the firewood. Victor?"

Victor nodded. "Yes."

CHAPTER
FORTY-ONE

"Chervet lied for you," said Tom.

"Yes."

"And he moved the pistol, next morning. You screwed up, didn't you? When you put it in her hand."

"Yes."

"And he saw that and he fixed it. And he lied about you being there. But he wouldn't stay there with you, would he? Wouldn't stay at Dead Horse. He left with your wife's body and he never came back."

"He wanted to go home."

"Can't say I blame him. Maybe he figured that sooner or later, you'd want to get rid of the only witness."

"It was an accident. Victor knew that."

"Pretty convenient accident."

"I loved her. I didn't want her dead. I didn't want…."

Limply, he raised his hand, made a small circling motion.

"I didn't want any of this."

Tom nodded. "What about the ranch hands? Ramirez and Archuleta. The bunkhouse is closer to the field than the ranch house. They didn't hear that plane come in?"

"They were paid off."

Tom sighed. "You coulda stayed. You know that, don't you? You coulda got yourself a good lawyer."

Whitfield's eyes narrowed. "Would you have believed me, Sheriff? Would you've believed it was an accident?"

"Probably not. But that's me. Jury's a different thing."

"I didn't want to take the chance. I was desperate. I was in shock – I wasn't thinking very clearly, Sheriff."

"Managed to fly that plane all the way back to Los Angeles."

"It doesn't take much to fly a plane, once you know how."

"And afterward, you went back to your hotel room, and you waited for me to call."

"I didn't wait for anything. I passed out as soon as I got to the room."

"But you knew somebody'd call. Sooner or later."

"Sooner or later, yes."

"And all these years you been living with this."

"Yes."

"And so has Mrs. Whitfield's daughter."

"Yes. I feel badly about the girl."

"Damn sweet of you."

"Do you want to take a punch at me, Sheriff? Will that make you feel better?"

"I'm tempted," said Tom. "But tell me something."

Raoul cleared his throat. "What?"

"Why'd you fly out there that particular night? Why then?"

• • •

Dead Horse was abandoned.

Tom parked the Dodge by the entrance to the adobe wall that encircled the ranch house. The wall's gate was hanging at an angle – the hinge at the top had rusted loose. He stared out across the sun burnt grass to the house itself. The windows were boarded over. In the silence, far off, he could hear the long rattling whirr of a cicada.

He walked along the road, and then alongside the polo field. Between the weeds, there was still a path leading to the big piñon and the empty bleachers. He followed it, and then sat down on the lowest bench and looked out at the gently waving tops of the grasses and the wild flowers.

Ten years ago, he had been sitting exactly here when he first talked with Raoul Whitfield.

Ten years ago, two days before Tom met with him, Raoul Whitfield had killed his wife.

Once again, he remembered the woman as he had seen her that long-ago Fourth of July. Slender and agile in her lemon yellow dress, her face bright, her eyes sparkling, as she handed the cotton candy to her daughter.

173

He pictured her as she must have been after Whitfield left for California. Wandering around in the empty house, probably with a drink in her hand. Alone except for Chervet. Reminders of a happier life all around her, furniture and books and clothes, everything poisoned now by betrayal.

Wounded, downhearted, using alcohol to fog the day, sleeping pills to dodge the night.

He pictured her lying on that bed when Whitfield came into the room that night. He pictured her going for the gun.

Would she really have shot him?

Didn't matter now.

He heard a car, looked up, and saw a big Buick driving toward him.

The car stopped and Murray Carleton got out. In a nicely-cut three-piece suit he came ambling down the path to the bleachers, around the trunk of the piñon. When he reached Tom, he pulled out his pocket watch and glanced at it.

"I can't stay long," he said. "I need to get back to Santa Fe tonight."

"Won't take long," Tom told him. "Have a seat."

Carleton slipped the watch back into his pocket and sat down.

"You hear about Lois Bell?" Tom asked him.

"I read about her. Poor girl."

"I went out to California, talked to Raoul."

"Did you?" said Carleton, politely interested.

"He told me about flying out to the ranch that night. Told me about killing Mrs. Whitfield."

Carleton looked puzzled. "Emily? Raoul killed Emily?"

"An accident, he says. But he made a mistake. He didn't put the Colt in her hand the right way. Chervet figured that out, next morning, and he took the pistol away."

"Are you saying that Victor Chervet was in league with Raoul?"

Tom smiled. "Forget it," he said. "It all over."

"What on earth are you talking about?"

Tom reached into his shirt pocket, took out a folded sheet of paper, held it up.

"It's all in here," he said. "How you called him the day before, told him about Emily changing her will. Whitfield says it was you

174

who suggested he come out here and talk to Emily."

"Absurd."

"Thing is, you even told me you'd talked to her that day. The day before she died. Never occurred to me that she'd mentioned the will to you. I'm a little slow on the uptake sometimes."

"She told me no such thing."

"It's all in here," said Tom, and slipped the paper back into his pocket.

"And even if I had informed Raoul," said Carleton, "which I didn't, there's no law against it."

"There's a law against concealing evidence of a crime. You knew that Raoul was going out there that night. He told you he'd be borrowing a plane. Just to be on the safe side, you set yourself up with Lois Bell, got yourself an alibi."

"Why would I need an alibi?"

"Like I say, you talked to Mrs. Whitfield. Maybe she told you how angry she was. Maybe she even told you she'd shoot her husband if she ever saw him again."

Carleton smiled. "Again, even if she had, why would I need an alibi?"

"In case something happened. To Emily or to Whitfield. I figure you're the kind of guy likes to cover his bets."

"Nonsense."

"What happened was, Raoul killed her. And you used your influence with Peter Alonzo to close the case, call it a suicide."

"This is absolute nonsense. Even if any of it were true, which it isn't, there's virtually no way I could've predicted that Raoul would shoot Emily."

"Not predict it, no. But you like to manipulate people, see what happens, see if you can turn it to your own advantage. And it all worked out pretty well for you, didn't it?"

"Sheriff, I have absolutely no idea what you're talking about."

"I'm guessing it was you who set up Lois and Whitfield in the first place. You introduced the two of 'em, didn't you? Just before you passed out – or pretended to pass out – in the Cantina. You figured that if Whitfield got involved with Lois, a woman you knew, you'd maybe have some leverage over him."

"Leverage? To do what?"

"Whatever you wanted. Get 'em to play your little games.

Whitfield told me all about the games. The drugs, all the rest of it."

"Nonsense."

"And I figure it was you called Mrs. Whitfield that February and told her that her husband was over at Lois's place. The night she went over there and found him. Probably disguised your voice, so she wouldn't know it was you."

"And why would I tell Emily about Lois?"

"You knew she was a jealous woman. You knew how she'd react. You figured that if you could split them up, the Whitfields, you'd get something out of it for yourself."

"And what exactly would that be?"

"Raoul. You wanted Raoul. And you were right. You got him. And at the end of the day, you got all the rest of it, too." He waved his hand toward the piñon, the polo field, the ranch house. "All belongs to you now, doesn't it?"

"This is all wild speculation. I hope, for your sake, that you haven't mentioned this to anyone. I do know my way around the slander laws."

Tom shook his head. "Thought we'd have a little talk first, you and me."

"You do realize that none of this would stand up in court."

"Probably not. Look real good in the newspapers, though. Really help out that campaign of yours."

Carleton frowned. "Sheriff, you may not like me, but I've become a man of some importance in this state. I can be useful to you."

Tom smiled. "Doubt it. Planning to retire soon. Figure you should do the same."

"What?"

"You're right. I don't like you. Not at all. And I don't want to see you as governor. You pull out, you withdraw from the race. And I'll keep this to myself." He tapped the paper in his shirt pocket.

"You're insane."

"Like you say, there's not much I can do to you, legally. But I can stop you from being governor. One way or the other. You withdraw, I hold on to this. You keep running, I give it to the newspapers."

176

Carleton looked at him for a moment, then rose from the bench, strode a few paces away, toward the big piñon tree. He stood there with his back to Tom.

Tom rose from the bench, watching him, his right hand hanging free alongside his Colt.

Slowly, Carleton turned to face him. "What if I can prove to you that virtually none of this ever happened?"

"Be interesting."

Carleton began to reach inside his coat.

Tom held up his left hand. "Wait."

Carleton's hand stopped moving.

"You sure you want to do that?" Tom asked him. "You may be hot stuff in the Gun Club, Mr. Carleton, but I've been using this Colt for over thirty years. Before you clear that holster, you'll be dead."

Carleton stood there, staring at him. His hand was still poised at the opening of his jacket.

"Someone'll find the body sooner or later," said Tom. "I'll be the one who investigates. Probably turn out to be another one of those senseless killings."

Carleton's hand trembled.

"You leave the race," said Tom, "You make the announcement today. And I'll keep this to myself." With the fingertips of his left hand, he tapped again at the paper in his pocket.

"Why am I dropping out?" said Carleton. "What's my excuse?"

"Health reasons." Tom smiled bleakly. "Close enough to the truth."

Slowly, Carleton's hand moved down to his side. He lowered his head.

Tom nodded. "Good thinking," he said.

Carleton turned and moved away, his walk slower now, his head still lowered.

Tom watched him shamble down the pathway, get into the Buick, start it, drive away. He didn't look at Tom.

Tom slipped the sheet of paper from his pocket, opened it. It was just as empty as it was when it put it there, back at the office.

He let out his breath.

CHAPTER
FORTY-TWO

Yes, Ma'am," said Tom into the telephone.

"He actually admitted that he killed her?" said Miss Templeton.

Tom sat back in his office chair. "Yes, Ma'am. Said it was an accident. I'm inclined to believe him."

"Will there be a trial?"

"No. He won't testify. And there's no evidence. But at least we know now, for a fact, that it wasn't suicide. I'd be real grateful if you told the girl."

"Of course. Of course I will. You say he has tuberculosis?"

"And a few other things. Won't be lasting much longer."

"In a way, you know, I feel almost sorry for him."

"He came back here, Ma'am, because he knew he was gonna get cut from her will. He says he wanted her back, but I think what he wanted was the life she gave him."

"Aren't you being a little hard, Sheriff?"

"Maybe so. But he could've let the girl know. Any time over the past ten years, he could've done something. Written an anonymous letter. Done something."

"Yes. Yes, I suppose he could have."

"He doesn't get much sympathy from me."

"I understand."

"Anyway. Figured you and the girl should know."

"Sheriff, I can't tell you how grateful I am."

"My pleasure, Miss Templeton. I'm happy I can do it."

"I'll get in touch with her as soon as I can."

"Thank you, Ma'am."

"And your daughter, Sheriff? Maria? How is she doing?"

"Just fine. This week, she wants to be a doctor."

178

"Good for her."

"Yes, Ma'am. Well. Good luck to you. And you take care now."

"You, too, Sheriff. And God bless you."

Tom hung up, sat back.

Watched the summer breeze flutter the pale blonde hair, ruffle the hem of the lemon yellow dress. Watched the daughter solemnly take the cone of spun sugar, small white fingers gently curling around it.

He leaned forward again, lifted the phone's receiver, clicked the button, got Monica at the exchange, gave her an Albuquerque number.

The phone rang and rang. Finally someone answered in a young female voice that Tom didn't recognize. "Hello?"

"Hello. Could I talk to Maria Delgado, please?"

"Who's calling?"

"Her father."

"Okay. Hang on."

After a moment, Maria came on the line. "Daddy?"

"Hi, Sweetie."

"What's up? Is something wrong?"

"No. I was just thinking –"

Someone knocked at Tom's door.

"Hold on for a second," he told her. He put his hand over the receiver's mouthpiece and called out, "Come in."

Phil Sanchez poked his head into the door. "Tom, you hear what happened?"

"What?"

"It's Murray Carleton. He's dropping out of the race — he just made an announcement."

"He say why?"

"His health, he said. Jesus, he had the thing all wrapped up. Weird, huh?"

"Yeah. Thanks, Phil."

Sanchez ducked back out, pulled the door shut.

Tom took his hand off the mouthpiece. To Maria he said, "I was thinking about coming down there tomorrow, maybe taking you out to dinner."

"Oh, Daddy, that'd be great. What was that all about? There at your office?"

"What?"

"Just now. When you had your hand over the phone."

"Oh. Business, Sweetie. Nothing for you to worry about."

ACKNOWLEDGMENTS

A lot of people helped with this book. In Santa Fe, years ago, it was Melanie Peters who first told me the story. For a time, her real estate company held Dead Horse Ranch among its listings.

Thanks to Lynne and Peter Coneway, who currently own Dead Horse, and who filled out the story and let me wander around the property. Thanks to Cathi Lewis, who knows the property and its history, and who told me quite a lot about both.

Thanks to the patient people at the San Miguel County Clerk's office in Las Vegas, New Mexico, who tolerated my endless prowling through their records. Thanks also to Peg Mortimer in Albuquerque and Petey Salmon in Las Vegas. They personally knew Raoul and Emily and Lois, and they were generous with their time and knowledge. Wit Slick, who runs the terrific Plaza Hotel in Las Vegas, not only has a great name, but he's a great guy, helpful and kind. Diana Stein, who owns Los Artesanos Bookstore, is both those things as well, and she provided important background information about the town, a rare photo of Lois and Raoul, and a summary of Emily's will.

Thanks to Peter Ruber, Otto Penzler, William F. Nolan, and Rick Layman for providing valuable tidbits about Raoul, his writing, and his wives.

Thanks to Brad Spurgeon, of the *International Herald Tribune*, for information about Paris.

Other people provided various specialized kinds of help. Dr. Roger Smithpeter helped with the medical information; George Adelo with the legal information; retired Air Force trainer Billy Harvey, and *St. Petersburg Times* reporter Jean Heller, with the aviation information. None of them, of course, are responsible for any errors of mine.

Three people – Richard Brenner, Jonathan Richards, and Tilo Eckhardt – read early versions of the manuscript, and they all offered valuable suggestions.

§

Raoul, Emily, and Lois were all real people, and the trajectories of their respective lives were as given in the book. At the time he met Emily in France, Raoul was one of the most famous, and probably one of the best paid, mystery writers in the country.

Emily's wounds, and the events of her death, were as given. The local newspapers of the time all implied that she had been murdered, and that the truth of her death was being covered up.

Victor Chervet, the ranch manager, did accompany Emily's body to New York, and was never seen again.

Murray Carleton was a real person, one not unlike the character in this book, but he was not Raoul's lawyer, and so far as I know, he never planned to run for governor of New Mexico.

There was no Sheriff Tom Delgado.

So far as we know, Raoul never admitted any responsibility for the death of Emily Whitfield.